ELÉCTRICO

W

ELÉCTRICO W

HERVÉ LE TELLIER

TRANSLATED BY ADRIANA HUNTER

OTHER PRESS

New York

Library of Congress Cataloging-in-Publication Data
Le Tellier, Hervé, 1957-
[Eléctrico W. English]
Eléctrico W / by Hervé Le Tellier ; translated by Adriana Hunter.
   p. cm.
"Originally published in French in 2011 by Jean-Claude Lattès,
Paris, France."
   ISBN 978-1-59051-533-4 (pbk.) — ISBN 978-1-59051-534-1 (ebook)
1. Journalists—Fiction.   2. Translators—Fiction.   3. French—
Portugal—Lisbon—Fiction.   4. Photographers—Portugal—
Lisbon—Fiction.   5. Interpersonal relations—Fiction.   I. Hunter,
Adriana.   II. Title.
   PQ2672.E11455E4413 2012
   843'.914—dc23

2012026349

If I can stop one heart from breaking
I shall not live in vain
If I can ease one life the aching
Or cool one pain
Or help one fainting robin
Unto his nest again
I shall not live in vain.

——EMILY DICKINSON

When I tried taking off the mask,
It stuck to my face.
When I pulled it off and looked in the mirror,
I'd grown older.

——FERNANDO PESSOA

PROLOGUE OF SORTS

We were heading toward Rossio in a taxi the color of olives, green and black, an ancient Mercedes 220, one of those rounded sedans from the sixties. It was still summer but a gray Atlantic rain was falling and the sky was pewter-colored. Lisbon did not look itself, but the setting may not matter very much. Water streamed over the car window, Antonio gazed out at the city, not concentrating on anything for long. I thought he seemed transparent, absent and present all at the same time—a watermark in the weft of a sheet of paper.

As the taxi slowed to turn into the square by Eduardo VII Park, Antonio took a pack of cigarettes from his pocket and struck a match. He inhaled, sucking in his cheeks, and wound down the window to blow out a scroll of smoke

snatched away as we sped along. I mention these insignificant details, not much more than snapshots, because they
struck me so emphatically, as did the suffocating smell of
sulfur and tobacco.

It felt as if time had taken a step to one side, a divergence
as fine as a crack in the glaze on porcelain. Something
unfamiliar had insinuated itself inside me. I can think of
no other way of putting it: I no longer saw a thirty-year-
old man in flesh and blood sitting beside me on that seat
with its cracked leather, but a character, a character from
a book.

That same evening I made the decision to write it. I
didn't let my ignorance of the plot or framework hold me
back. I had no Ariadne's thread, I just took my big black
notebook from my bag and wrote these few sentences, in
the past tense, exactly as they appear here, I have left them
unchanged.

People will suspect some sort of imposture, a feeble
writer's strategy. They would be wrong: there was actually nothing extraordinary, fascinating, or, in a nutshell,
bookworthy about Antonio Flores. Physically he was
ordinary, although his brown, almost curly hair tended
toward auburn. His dark eyes were mischievous without
being playful, and cutting down his forehead between his
thick eyebrows he had two vertical lines that gave him
an alert expression. His legs looked too short to me, and
he seemed more elegant sitting than standing. If he had

to walk quickly, a childhood injury made him limp. And yet he had indisputable charm, his own particular way of occupying space, what people call magnetism.

There was nothing predictable or expected about Antonio Flores. Never, in the nine days I spent with him, was I so much as a comma ahead of the sentences that his presence provoked. Never, right up until the collapse, did I guess where Antonio was taking me. He himself knew nothing about this extraordinary phenomenon. His every move conformed to some invisible scheme, and certain silences dictated the beginning of a new paragraph.

So here begins the book. I have revised it—very little, to be honest—as I typed it up. I altered some turns of phrase because they no longer conveyed the exact feeling of the moment in which they were conceived. It was 1985, nearly twenty-seven years ago. At the time I didn't feel like showing it to publishers. I did give it a title, though, and this morning, with the sun taking its time coming up, it is still called *Eléctrico W*, the name of a tramline in Lisbon. But that has been a provisional title for so long.

This paragraph is added in because, according to the computer, the manuscript comprised 53,278 words. I wanted it to be a prime number. Out of some superstition. So I added an adjective here, an adverb there, I don't even remember where. And this is where the notebook starts again.

DAY ONE

ANTONIO

*J*ust as we reached Rossio Square along the Avenida da Liberdade, it stopped raining, and the Mercedes dropped us at the terrace of a bistro. The chairs were soaked, the table too; we carelessly put our two suitcases down in puddles. As the waiter took our orders, he glanced at our luggage in dismay, or simply indifference.

Antonio and I had never worked together but we had come across each other several times. His photos had illustrated my investigation into the *garimpeiros*, destitute gold miners in the Orinoco Basin; I'd written a piece to go with his reportage on the tribes of Botswana's Okavango Delta. When he decided to go back to Lisbon for this particular series of articles, it was his idea to suggest me to his editors. He thought I was still living in Paris, and when he learned that I was now the newspaper's Portuguese correspondent, he said these words (so odd that they were relayed to me): "I knew his fate would bring him to Lisbon at some point."

I had only been here a few months. I had wanted to leave Paris, to avoid the risk of bumping into Irene in the corridors of the editorial department, to recover from my absurd love for this girl with her outdated name, this girl who didn't want me. My father's death in late June, his suicide—why not use the word—had made up my mind. My brother and I had sold the apartment on the rue Lecourbe, and with my share of the proceeds I had decided to buy a one-bedroom apartment in either the Castelo quarter or Santa Justa, where my mother was born and where I had spent a few holidays as a child. In the meantime, I had rented a studio in São Paulo, right next to the goods port. It was a huge room which afforded few comforts but it was whitewashed and sunny, at the top of a three-story building. It was the views more than anything that had attracted me. From one window you could look out over the roofs, from the other you could see the Tagus. The bed was new and comfortable, and there was a phone line connected. There was a small open-plan kitchen and a shower, but the toilet was in the hallway. "For substantial things . . . ," the landlady had explained, then, gesturing toward the sink, she chuckled, "but for anything else, okay?" In her view, a refrigerator and two hotplates justified the label studio. The compressor on the fridge made more noise than a factory press, and I soon had to settle for unplugging it at night.

I had hung my only picture on the wall, and that was just a dog-eared, yellowed copy of a late-nineteenth-century map of the Okavango Delta. I had set up my desk in a corner, which was blocked on one side. I put my fax on it and this cube-shaped computer with its small black-and-white screen, whose successors I could never have imagined. Sitting there, I could look through the window to my right and see the docks. On nights when I couldn't sleep, in other words almost every night, I found their rumblings comforting. I left one window open and listened to the thunder of heavy diesel engines and fuel pumps, and the workers' cries and laughter. Sometimes I got up before dawn and wandered through the steely sadness of static and traveling cranes. Living in the entrails of a port felt nostalgic and reassuring, like those English paintings of industrial landscapes, all in grays and blues. And Lisbon, a capital open to the seas, seemed to blend exoticism with civilization.

I had set myself two tasks for the imminent autumn: to finish the novel about Pescheux d'Herbinville for which I had only written a few pages and chosen a title (*The Clearing*), then to translate Jaime Montestrela's *Contos aquosos*, the collection of bizarre short stories that he subtitled *Atlas inutilis*. Montestrela was far from well known, but at a secondhand bookstall in the Alfama neighborhood I had stumbled across a copy of his *Contos* and was instantly drawn to the whiff of dark humor they gave off. It was a thick volume, but these ironic and fantastical short stories were barely a few lines long, with a darkness reminiscent of Max Aub or Roland Topor. Out of almost a thousand, I had already translated about a hundred. Here is the first one I chanced on, the day I happened to open the book. It is a pretty good illustration of Montestrela's mindset:

Centuries before our era, Mongols of the Ouchis tribe worshipped an adolescent named Ohisha who, when he reached puberty, stopped aging. Fascinated by this phenomenon, they soon made him their leader. The young man did, however, die at the age of seventy-three. The legend of Ohisha ended with these words: "Lying on his shroud he was still identical to himself. For all those years, only his body had aged terribly."

I hadn't got very far with this work when Antonio Flores called. He asked me to move in with him for a fortnight to follow the Pinheiro trial, and I was happy to bring an end to my isolation. I didn't give up the room, I had adopted my own routine there. Antonio booked a hotel on the rua Primeiro de Dezembro in the center of town. It was quite expensive, but the paper was picking up the bill.

The Pallazo Meiras, which dated back to the early 1900s, was both tired-looking and luxurious. This palace must once have had some appeal, but renovations had reduced it to one of those international havens where you never feel at home, and don't even want to unpack your bags. As I walked through the door I felt I had stepped into a strange ship washed up in the middle of the city, a steamer in pink marble and gray stone. The staff went about their business languidly and managed to communicate their boredom to guests. The main entrance was draped with black-and-white-striped fabric and opened onto a small paved courtyard. In this funereal setting, despite his red livery, the footman looked like an undertaker waiting for a coffin to carry.

Antonio had booked two suites on the third floor. They were exact mirror images of each other, and the two lounges were connected by heavy double doors. Once we had opened these, the central room made more sense, with our bedrooms to either side. Antonio immediately dumped his equipment on a large carved oak desk, and I put my files on its twin. The brownish leather of two armchairs sat uncomfortably with the straw yellow of two more-rustic-looking chairs; the balconies looked out over Restauradores Square, and the noise was tolerable if we didn't open the windows.

It was ten years since Antonio had been in Lisbon. He had recently bought a tiny one-bedroom apartment in the old Belleville quarter of Paris, and I knew he had also lived in Rio, as well as spending a few months in London's Soho. He had made a name for himself in the small world of war photographers.

In the taxi on the way back from the airport, I asked why the long absence, and he just said, "A thing. A thing with a woman." We didn't exchange another word, and I regretted being so inquisitive. But that first evening, in a tasca in the port where we were having a last glass of bagaço, he started talking, in snippets, as if one memory led to another. From the emotion in his voice and the muddled way he confided in me, I suspected he had never opened up to anyone and could only do so at last because I was a foreigner. I let him talk.

ANTONIO FLORES IS ELEVEN, he lives in the old Bairro Alto quarter. Known as just Tonio, he is hurtling down the long flight of cement steps on the Travessa do Carmo. It is early May, the morning light is more blinding than golden. His schoolbag lurches in every direction on his back, buffeted from one shoulder to the other like a panicking rider on a runaway horse.

Every schoolday, Tonio races the Eléctrico W, which stops outside his house at 8:18 in the morning. Tonio had trouble getting up today, the 8:18 has already left and he's waiting for the 8:24. He will be late for school, for sure.

The Eléctrico W is the yellow-and-white funicular tram which carries its cargo of housewives and office workers every morning—except for Sundays and public holidays. True, it's ancient, but whatever the weather it trundles unfailingly from the old Bairro Alto quarter to the exhaust fumes and traffic jams of Baixa.

Several feet ahead of Tonio, the W rolls down the hill on its steel rails, making terrible metallic screeching sounds. The pantographs splutter with bright sparks against the azure sky, the traction cable at the back rises up from the rusted channel cut into the cement. Tonio runs behind it, keeping an eye on every sway of the cable, imagining it is the trailing black tail of a tired old dragon. In the rear of the carriage, a kid with a lollipop presses his grubby face against the steamed-up window and stares at Tonio, his empty eyes crushed by boredom.

Tonio runs. He knows every paving slab on the Travessa do Carmo, every stone, every porch: right on the corner the step is a bit high, you really have to stretch your leg to avoid tripping; here, to turn as sharply as possible, you can spin on the No Parking sign; there, on that street corner, it's better to slow up, last week he knocked down a smartly dressed old man coming out of a tasca. Of course, he could run just behind the W, on the concrete slope, but he's already fallen once, catching his shoe in the rim of the rail, and it hurt too much. It left him with a scar as white and shiny as a trail of salt, and the pharmacist, Mr. Pereira, claimed he would have a mark there "till the day he died." The thought of his own death—he was only six at the time—terrified him and he started crying. His mother kissed him to comfort him, and turned angrily on the pharmacist: "Mr. Pereira, really! What sort of thing is that to say to a child?"

With all this reminiscing, the W has got a little way ahead, and Tonio runs like a boy possessed.

"Go on, Tonio, go on, faster, you've got to turn back time . . . ," laughs the fishmonger, and he lobs a hail of crushed ice at the boy, its smell strong with seaweed and saltwater. Tonio ducks to avoid it and carries on with his race. Just ahead, the tram turns to the left and disappears around the corner. Tonio slows abruptly, skids in the dust and gravel, and comes to a stop, breathless.

This is because, after the corner, the steps come to an end, and with them the Travessa do Carmo's narrow sidewalk. The W forks off and continues on its way alone in the clear cool shade of a narrow corridor between buildings. Deadened by the shuttered facades, the noise drops, becomes muffled. At the end, fifty paces farther, the dark mouth of a tunnel gapes, and when the tram enters it, the neon lights in the cabin and the round red taillight come on. In the underground darkness, sparks fly from the catenaries, lighting up the curve of the vaulted ceiling like the thousand fires of hell in the illustrated Bible his aunt gave him.

The glowing sparks fade in the distance, the sound of the Eléctrico W is swallowed by the hubbub of the city, and Tonio hears someone behind him say, "Hey, you really run fast . . ."

She is seven years old, maybe eight, big black eyes, a straight nose. She has long dark hair, neatly smoothed. Tonio can't speak, he is still out of breath, his hair clinging to his sweating face.

She smiles.

"Well, my name's Duck, it is."

"What? What's your name?"

"Duck, like I said. Everyone calls me that. You can too, if you like, you can call me Duck. And what's your name?"

Tonio stays silent for a moment, rubbing his aching legs.

"Antonio . . . Well, Tonio. Do you live round here?"

She points to one of the buildings that look down over the W's route. Its white facade is dazzling in the sunlight, and Tonio screws up his eyes.

"Over there. You can't see it from here."

She lowers her arm and watches him with a pout. Tonio is intrigued, but he's also growing impatient.

"I have to go to school. I'm late. Aren't you?"

"Yes, yes, of course I'm late. Well then? Go on, keep running, go to school, if it's that important."

With a flick of her wrist she swishes her black hair over her shoulder. Tonio doesn't know this yet but it's a woman's gesture.

"Do you run after the Eléctrico like that every day? I've never seen you."

"Usually it's the eighteen minutes past."

"Really?"

She sits down on a large granite bollard, playing with the dust with the tip of her sandal.

"And will you be late again tomorrow?" she asks.

"No, I'll be on time tomorrow."

"So we won't see each other again. That's your bad luck. Well, hi from Duck."

She stands up and runs off, and Tonio watches her until she turns the corner at the top of the street and disappears.

The next day Tonio left late again. The little girl was there, on the bollard. She had already let one W go by, and had left her mother wondering why she had got up so early.

FOR HIS FIFTEENTH birthday, Tonio is given a camera, a Russian Zenit E which is cheap and temperamental, nothing is automatic and it weighs as much as an iron. His family insists he take his first picture. He refuses. It will be of Duck.

A LITTLE LATER, one January morning, it snows in Lisbon. Tonio is waiting for Duck at the huge viewpoint on the rua Santa Catarina which overlooks the docks and the port. Duck is late, and Tonio is hopping from one foot to the other, wearing an old fur-lined jacket given to him by his father, it makes him look like a soldier. Duck is now thirteen, she is almost as tall as he is, although he's nearly sixteen, and her youthful face already radiates a more unsettling beauty. Tonio still calls her Duck, has never stopped calling her that. He is cold, really cold, he stamps his feet on the frozen ground. In the distance, on the icy, muddy waters of the Tagus, the ferry heading for Barreiro passes the one arriving from Seixal and salutes it with a blast of its horn.

Antonio waits. Duck has been late before, but this morning he feels a new twinge of anxiety, an inexplicable but mild apprehension. It is market day and he lets his eye roam over the crowd of passersby. He thinks he spots her a hundred times, in a flyaway lock of hair, the pattern on a dress, a stranger's gait. Every time he gets that fleeting quiver, that constriction deep inside him, and each time the disappointment. The waiting feels easier because of this endlessly impatient searching.

All at once, woolen fingers warm with life come and cover his face, startling him.

"Don't turn around," she says. "Close your eyes."

He obeys with a smile. The woolen fingers slip away. He can guess, Duck is in front of him, her breath is chocolaty, blowing warmly over his chin.

"Make sure your eyes are closed, don't cheat."

The fingers slide over his temples, into his hair, gently drawing him closer. Tonio's lips feel the touch of other lips, that open slightly. He stops breathing and opens his eyes, just as Duck closes hers, he has never seen them from so close, those long eyelashes resting on the soft pink of her cheeks. She pushes him away, just a little, then presses herself to him again.

"You looked," she whispers in his ear.

She pulls away, takes him by the hand and drags him toward the railing of the viewpoint. Snowflakes twirl around them, catching in their hair as it flies in the wind, it is a north wind, blowing a little harder now. On the Tagus, the ferry from Barreiro goes into reverse, its propellers churning the dirty water into shining creamy whirlpools. Tonio looks lost, helpless, he wishes he could talk but can't manage a single word. Duck comes over to him and puts her arms around him. Then she takes off her gloves and slips her hands into his.

"Warm me up, Tonio, I'm cold."

Duck's fingers touch his, squeeze them. Something's different. Tonio's eyes cloud over, he turns to look at her, but she puts a finger over his mouth and he knows he mustn't speak.

All she says is, "Tonio . . . I'm a woman, today."

He doesn't understand.

"I'm a woman," she repeats.

She spoke the words softly, and Tonio senses that she wants to lead him into another world, a world too big for him, and mysterious too, a world deeper than the sea, and he wants to follow her there, in spite of everything. Then he wants to speak, to let out all the words welling up inside him, but she kisses him again, he holds her to him: it is their first true kiss.

THE NIGHT SHE was fifteen, Duck met up with Tonio. It was one of those luminous stifling August nights scattered with shooting stars you could almost hear whistling through the sky. Tonio and Duck took cover in the W's tunnel because the next day was Sunday and the tram doesn't run on Sundays. They lay down on the air mattress Tonio had blown up and spread with a big thick bedcover that smelled of bleach and lavender. A family of bats lived in the roof but Tonio made sure they wouldn't do them any harm.

"You'll still have to protect me, Tonio."

She presses herself to him. She has put a drop of perfume on the back of her neck, and Tonio breathes in its musk and dark fruits.

They stay like that for a long time, not daring to talk, and it is in that position that they fall asleep. In the morning, when the dawning day sends long shadows into the tunnel, they make love, with trusting awkwardness. Everything is new, their bodies so alive they don't exist.

AT THIS POINT Antonio's voice cracked and he sat in silence. For a moment I hoped he had invented the story. I was jealous, felt as miserable as a vagrant who has wandered by mistake into the summer garden of an Eastern prince and, in his filthy tattered state, has to drift among its marble fountains, its orange trees and date palms. Antonio finished his brandy and we headed back to the hotel, walking slowly. He was shivering in the warm night air. I gathered he wasn't lying.

Duck was pregnant. "I'll kill him," her father bellowed, "do you hear me? I'll kill him." She wanted to run away, join Tonio, but her father caught up with her in the street and beat her to the ground, in front of the neighbors, with hideous words, and every time he struck her she picked herself up and cried, "I'm not ashamed, I'm not ashamed, you can't make me feel ashamed."

That same evening Duck was confined to the house, then sent far away, hidden with an elderly cousin in Braga by all accounts, and Antonio had to leave Lisbon. I couldn't understand this sudden fury. Was it all that catastrophic? Of course, Antonio told me. Abortion and pregnancy outside marriage were unthinkable. This was the 1970s, the calamitous closing phase of the *Estado novo*, the years of Salazar's dictatorship, and of a rural Portugal that has now been forgotten but was fervently behind Salazar, Roman Catholic and illiterate. Sister Maria Lucia of the Immaculate Heart was reverentially interviewed on television as she blew out her sixty candles at her Carmelite convent, because she had once been Lucia Dos Santos, one of the three child seers of Fatima to whom the Blessed Virgin appeared six times in 1917. Yes, those were the days of the three F's: Fatima, fado, and football.

Antonio left for Paris, where an uncle took him in. First he sold newspapers, then he learned to draw and perfected his photographic skills.

"I'll always wait for you," Duck had promised, and from his Paris exile Antonio wrote dozens of letters that he sent to a mutual friend. A few weeks later Duck's father and his wife moved house, it was even said they moved out of Lisbon. Neither Antonio nor anyone else ever had news of Duck again. I asked no more questions.

We were still walking, the street had turned into a staircase and Antonio fell silent again, his eyes lowered. With his thumb he stroked a very narrow ring, a ring so simple that—I am quite sure of it now—it can only have been made of copper, perhaps even a curtain ring. I knew that, at that same moment and wherever she was, on Duck's left hand there was an identical wedding ring with the same red glint.

WE PARTED WITHOUT a word in the hotel corridor. I opened my door as he was putting his key into his lock, I gave him a last friendly wave, and took a few steps into my room.

For a split second, in the half light, I thought I recognized my reflection in a huge mirror to my left. But something was not right. This double seemed to have a life of his own, and I realized that, each through our own doors, Antonio and I had walked into the single lounge we had created between our two bedrooms. We took the same steps, made the same moves.

Antonio turned on a lamp, on autopilot, without noticing me there, and I caught the absent look his eye. I recognized the gaze of a man quite alone, drifting, far from his wife and child, a look of pure distress, of someone lost. I knew I had trespassed into his pain, and felt still more naked than he was, and also appallingly unhelpful, hungry for his sincerity, devoid of affection, rapacious as a chronicler of his suffering.

He noticed me, pulled himself together and gave a joyless smile before retiring to his bedroom and closing the door behind him.

THAT NIGHT, as I often did, I thought back to the life my father had resolved to leave behind, a grim gray life. I may have been wrong—it's true that other people's happiness is mind-numbingly boring—but I felt he had gone through life without the tiniest spark of incident. He was twenty just before the Second World War, but he was not a Resistance fighter, nor even a collaborator. He had absolutely no secret double life, or longing for adventure, absolutely no fifteen minutes of fame. Now that he was definitively dead, I took the step of resenting him for this, of wishing some of his glow could have cast light on my own life.

But it was memories of Irene that stopped me getting to sleep.

The first time I saw her was at the newspaper's archives. She was standing there smoking, leaning out of the window. Most women conceal their bodies with clothes, Irene used them to draw attention to her nakedness under them. Her black dress revealed her slender shoulders and showed off her back. The fine material hugged her buttocks and hips, and her lovely breasts seemed to be making a bid for independence. Her mouth was half open, her lips full, almost maddening, gleaming pale pink. A hint of abandon in her movements and of color in her cheeks suggested someone had just made love to her, a languid look in her eye that she wanted it to be done again and again. She asked me what article I was looking for, I had already forgotten. At first I thought I just wanted her, violently; I soon realized that I loved her, hopelessly.

At that time of the evening, Irene was most likely drinking her tea as usual at the Saint-Elme, the bar on the rue des Abbesses where she "entertained." It was her "salon," she claimed. She used to make herself comfortable on the banquette at the far end of the room, always with two books, one essay, one novel, and that notebook I've hardly ever seen her write anything in at all. Her brown curls were carelessly held up with pins, and she was always careful to let a few locks escape, in an artful arrangement. With the black shawl that she wore in the evenings, whatever the time of year, she looked like a fortune-teller.

I had seen her at the Saint-Elme several times, rarely with the same men. When she introduced me to them—if she even did introduce me—it made her laugh that she sometimes barely knew their names. But these passing characters, who had probably noticed she was free and had only just approached her, enjoyed an intimacy I was never granted. I would stick around, at first just for a moment, and then for too long, in the hope she would make up her mind to get up from the table and come with me, but I was always the one to give up the fight, leaving her to enjoy her new catch. I always regretted giving in to my urge to see her, and trying to plead for so much as a smile from her, and I pictured her leaving with those men, giving herself to them, like a bitch in heat, yes, that was the expression that came to mind, with images to match. One evening she sat there with a tall, slightly balding man in glasses, "Stanislas, no, sorry, Ladislas," who was giving her a boring lecture about "natural foods," and I went home humiliated, crazed with impotent rage, and stubbed my cigarette out in the palm of my hand so that this pain would wipe out the other—in vain. The following day, when, with a note of anxiety in my voice, I tried to find out where and how the evening with Ladislas had ended, she was incensed by my questions. In the end, because I persisted clumsily and failed to disguise my own torment, she snapped in exasperation: "What do you want? To know if I slept with Lad, is that it? By what right, for God's sake? Yes, if you must know, all night, he fucked me and fucked me again, do you want details?" Her coarseness hit the target, mortifying me, and even the cruel intimacy of that "Lad" was calculated to hurt me. But I shrugged, looked away, and fled, only to come back and apologize later.

So, as with every incidence of insomnia, I translated a few more *Contos aquosos*. My lifeline. Jaime Montestrela wrote them over a period of three or four years at a rate of one a day. It was his "daily exercise," as he said in his "logbook." He often copied out the day's story and mailed it to someone, making a note of the addressee. Of the five I translated that night, I remembered the shortest, dedicated to a "Jacques B., in Paris":

On the island of Tahiroha, on Good Friday, cannibals who have converted to Christianity eat only sailors.

I had found very little information about Montestrela, even at the Biblioteca Nacional. He was born in Lisbon in 1925, and belonged to that generation of Portuguese writers from the time of the dictatorship, an era that included Augusto Abaleira and Eugénio de Andrade, whom he may have known. After studying medicine, he embarked on a career as a psychiatrist at the Miguel Bombarda hospital in Lisbon, until 1950, when, under the name Jaime Caxias, he published a collection of activist poetry: *Prisão* (Prison). His pseudonym was not taken at random because Caxias was the place where political prisoners were tortured under Salazar's dictatorship. Montestrela was soon unmasked, arrested by La Pide, the political police, and brutally interrogated for a week before being released. He planned his escape. He took exile in Brazil in 1951 and settled in Rio de Janeiro, where he found a job at the Capo d'Oro hospital. It was here that he wrote *Nihil obstat*, his only novel, a searing work heavily inspired by Lawrence Sterne, and *Cidade de lama* (City of mud), a "bizarre and masterful essay about solitude and exile," as André Malraux would go on to write. It was also in Rio that he met another exile, the writer and critic Jorge de Sena, to whom he in fact dedicated *Cidade de lama*. In 1956 when the military regime took power in Brazil, the two friends set off in search of democracies once more. Jorge de Sena left for the United States and the University of Santa Barbara, and Jaime for France and Paris. In his small Belleville apartment, he wrote *Contos aquosos*, shortly before he died in 1975 of a ruptured aneurism after lunching with several writers, including Raymond Queneau. It is actually that detail, found in his brief obituary in *O Século*, that encouraged me to take an interest in him. I quickly checked that none of his work had been translated into French, and felt that these *Watery Tales* might make a good starting point.

I also tried to write a few lines of *The Clearing*, my novel that I kept putting off till later. I wanted to create the portrait of a man, Pescheux d'Herbinville, whose name would not have gone down in history had he not, on May 30, 1832, mortally wounded one of the greatest mathematical geniuses, Évariste Galois, who was then only twenty. Galois would die of peritonitis at Cochin hospital the following day. The night before the duel, with a sense of urgency, he jotted a sort of scientific will on a few loose sheets of paper, "publicly exhorting the mathmeticians

Jacobi or Gauss to give their opinion, not on the accuracy, but the importance of the theorems" he had found. And important they were: they would rank among the fundamental works on algebra and the theory of numbers. Ever since the day I had heard this legendary anecdote, it had fascinated me. At the age of twenty, on the eve of certain death, what things with a decisive impact on humanity could *I* have scrawled on a scrap of paper?

My pitiful hero, Pescheux d'Herbinville, was a sort of dandy whom some of Galois's biographers accused of working as a spy for Charles II's police. But there was nothing to prove this. It seems he and Évariste had been friends, but had fallen in love with the same woman, one Stéphanie-Félicie Poterin du Motel. So little is known about their story that there is plenty of scope for invention. I had made Pescheux an obscure petty noble rather taken with republicanism, a stupid, complacent man, which he no doubt was. Alongside his humdrum pointless existence, I wanted to depict the studious and tumultuous life of an Évariste driven by a passion for mathematics, the epitome of intelligence and youth. So the fictionalized biography of Pescheux was merely a pretext for a novel about mediocrity and a reflection on jealousy. It was an ambitious project, and I probably put too much store by it to get on with it properly. I took my inspiration for the opening passage from Stendhal's *Charterhouse of Parma*, hoping I would immediately be unmasked: "On May 30,

1832, the republican Pescheux d'Herbinville arrived at the clearing accompanied by a friend who had just loaded one of the two dueling pistols and informed him that, because his adversary, Évariste, had no witness with him, it would be Évariste who picked the firearm."

I had struggled to reach the fortieth page of my large black notebook; it measured eight inches by twelve, had the words *Registre Le Dauphin, France*, on the cover, and comprised two hundred pages marked out in quarter-inch squares. Yes— call it fetishism, superstition, or idiocy—I used the same notebooks as the legendary writer Romain Gary but didn't succeed in stringing together more than a few words.

DAY TWO

IRENE

he page stayed blank on that particular night. I went out and walked down to the river, to the black glint of the water, and I strolled along the banks, not really thinking about anything. I waited till dawn, till the first ferry drew in, the bars along the port opened, and water could be heard heating in percolators, before making up my mind to return to the hotel. I went back to bed, snoozed until ten in the morning, and let the racket on the street wake me. I found Antonio in the lobby, reading the *Jornal de Notícias* with no sign of impatience. He had his cameras around his neck, he must already have taken a few pictures. He was the one who suggested having lunch in the old port.

Just as we were about to leave the hotel, an attendant at reception waved Antonio over and handed him a message from a telephone call received that morning. Antonio glanced at it quickly, folded it in four without a word, and thrust it violently in his pocket, as if wishing it would disappear. But, because I was watching, he explained, "It's not from the paper. I think they've forgotten us already . . ."

He must have sensed I was still curious and felt our budding friendship deserved better than this evasive comment. He took the note back out of his pocket, read it more attentively, folded it again, and put it away. Then he smiled mischievously: "Sometimes going away's not such a bad idea . . . Out of sight but not out of mind."

"Yes, something like that. Or absence makes the flames burn brighter."

We left the hotel, heading slowly toward the port, and Antonio put film into his Leica.

"I'm going to shoot in black and white. There's not much light, but it's interesting light, I might get something out of it. What the paper's really interested in is the Pinheiro trial, but I've just read that it's been postponed for three days, so we can start with Lisbon."

I nodded agreement. We had no precise goal, I had made no appointments and didn't feel like working yet. To use the editor's rather worn expression, my articles needed to give a feel for the place. Antonio would provide the photos and pen-and-ink sketches. He had a talent for that sort of thing.

I wanted Antonio to make the decisions, but he was keen to talk about Paris, about the woman who had left the message for him. A spell had been broken. I didn't feel he was talking with any enthusiasm. He described her in bland terms, with no colors coming to the surface, not really haunted by any tender images. Why did Antonio talk about her so inadequately, given he had described Duck so well? Is it all that dangerous to mention your longing and admit to emotions? Every now and then he came to a stop, angled his lens at a street corner, a misshapen facade, a gap between two buildings, and released the shutter without much conviction.

Antonio didn't love this woman, and I thought of Irene again, and the memory of her terrifies me because it's everywhere in me, ready to spring up as soon as I'm alone, when all it really is is regret.

She had agreed to see me more than once, had accepted my tender advances, and, even though she rejected my too urgent desire every time, I like to think she always did so gently. She asked only that I be patient. I waited for her love to blossom, as she insisted it should. My feelings grew stronger by the day, and more painful too. I had fallen in love with every detail of her face, with her girlish grin, and even her cruelty.

Perhaps it was the distance she maintained that chained me to her, in the same way that the coolness I sensed in

Antonio must have been holding the woman I didn't know who called him from Paris.

One evening, tired of my persistence, Irene told me I had got everything wrong, she made fun of me: "I'm not going anywhere, I'm not leaving you. You and me, we don't exist. Anyway, there isn't anything going on between us." She was right. That was weeks ago. I realized life had played a hell of a trick on me, letting me come that close to happiness. I decided to get away from Paris.

As I write those words, I don't see them as shameless or out of place. I only mention my own despair the better to describe Antonio's indifference. These ideas came to me while he was talking about this woman, and because it was Antonio who inspired them they belong here.

We walked until we came to a Chinese restaurant. It had an international name, something like The Inn of a Thousand Rewards, The Peking Palace, or The Golden Lotus. I didn't make a note of it, I was overwhelmed with sadness. We were served a sickly rich chop suey, with broccoli drowning in monosodium glutamate, and, without even asking, were given knives and forks. But the exotic décor managed to offset the lack of chopsticks. I tried to steer the conversation toward literature, toward Jaime Montestrela, but Antonio had never heard of him, or even of Eugénio de Andrade. He borrowed my copy of *Contos aquosos*, opened it at random to page 324, and quickly read a story I had not yet translated.

On the island of Caladonga, the inhabitants conceived of a god whose existence never came into question even though this god was, alas, very small and fragile. Hence, when they had stirred sugar into their coffee and were putting their spoons back down, they checked carefully that the god was not on that particular part of the saucer. A deicide can happen so quickly.

"And how many of these are there?" Antonio asked, weighing up the book. "A thousand?"

"One thousand and seventy-three precisely. It's a strange number."

Antonio smiled, almost a smirk, and put the book down. He ate his food quickly, still talking volubly about nothing in particular. In the blackened pages of my notebook there are a few phrases grasped on the wing. Some notes are almost illegible, as if I wanted to forget that I would have to read through them at some point. Even so I remember that, aided and abetted by the beer, Antonio started talking about Paris and all the women he had known. He made my head spin with his drunken aphorisms, clichés, and settings from cheap airport fiction. I did not make scrupulous notes. I only remember "things that always look like what they are," and "true love, which comes straightaway or not at all," and also "words that can ruin everything."

I should have smiled at this string of pearls. I could have countered each of them with the exact opposite argument, given him examples of passions that bloomed after many years, others that flourished on quarreling. I came up with a new aphorism along the lines of "No aphorism tells the truth," which is at least as good as the paradox of the liar stating "Yes, I'm lying." What was that philosopher's name again, the one who was said to have died prematurely because he couldn't disentangle that contradiction? Philitas of Cos? Hippias of Elis?

Yes, I should have smiled. But what Antonio was saying very quickly became uncomfortable for me. His every half-dime maxim resonated like the implacable truth. True love comes straightaway or not at all. Yes. Things always look like what they are. Yes again.

I was angry. I would have preferred a more constant Antonio, a less frivolous one, one more upset to be here in this city that must have brought his past back to life. His confidences about his Parisian amorous adventures did nothing for me, they were like stains on a white sheet. I wanted him to tell me more about Duck. We were wasting time.

"Antonio?"

He looked up.

"And . . . that woman, Duck? Don't you want to see her again?"

He said nothing for a long while.

"I don't know . . . We were just kids. She might just remember. I can't be sure she was really pregnant, or even, if she was, whether she had the baby. But I'm sure she has a husband now, and a life. And she could have written to me, if she really wanted to."

"Do you think? Would it have been possible?"

He wouldn't meet my eye, and I felt I understood.

"You're afraid of what you might find. Your Duck could be ugly now, or stupid. Maybe she already was, but you were—what—sixteen, seventeen? Over the years we dress everything up so much."

Antonio smiled. He took an old leather wallet with splitting seams from his jacket.

"Here."

He handed me a very tattered photograph, its colors faded, protected by a sheet of tracing paper—a photo of a very young girl. She wasn't just beautiful, with her great mass of dark hair swept up off the nape of her neck; there was something else, something that hurt me but that I couldn't immediately put my finger on.

"Who took the picture? Did you?"

"Yes."

"How old was she?"

"Fifteen. Just fifteen."

I couldn't take my eyes off the photo. Duck was smiling at Antonio. He had caught her by surprise as she put her hair up, her eyes had a child's dazzling sincerity, an incredible tenderness, the simple happiness of being together. Yes, that was it, the power this picture had was the look in Duck's eye trumpeting the fact that Antonio was alive, was loved.

Buried in the depths of my suitcase, I too have a picture of a woman, it's of Irene. I captured her one morning, leaning over the balcony in our hotel room in Lombardy. The image is out of focus, but in the background you can make out Lake Como, still blanketed in mist, Tremezzina Bay, the cypress trees, and the mountains and forests beyond. The balcony is red with climbing magnolias, it's going to be a gorgeous day, it's April.

Irene is looking at me too, she's surprised, but where's the tenderness? I'm not convinced by those beginnings of a smile, her eyes are cold, I'm an inconvenience to her, useless, she wishes she were alone to make the most of this tranquillity and enjoy the view. Because of that photograph and that blank, empty, Medusa-like expression, I sometimes even wonder whether, whenever a couple books a room with a view, there's always one who watches the other while the other just wants to admire the view.

Looking at that face today, I know that a woman who could look at me like that could never have loved me. In fact, there's so little of anything in her eyes that I don't even think she looks attractive, and can't even remember why I wanted her so much. That's another reason the photo so rarely comes out of the suitcase.

Antonio has put the picture back in his wallet.

"You're right, it's true, I'm frightened. But not for the reasons you said. I'm frightened of coming back after all these years, of not meaning anything to her anymore, absolutely nothing. I couldn't bear it. I'd rather not hope. Besides, I never look at that photo. I don't even know why I still keep it on me."

He stopped talking, letting his gaze wander over the nearby Tagus. For a moment I doubted my convictions.

The silhouette of a willow tree rearing up halfway along the bank cut across the clouds. The tree must have been dead, gradually poisoned off by rust and engine grease. Its naked branches were rigid despite the breeze blowing in from the ocean. Just one waved feebly, like a survivor on a battlefield raising his arm among the corpses in the hope of being saved. I saw the seagull flying away. It had just taken off. The branch it had left a moment earlier had sprung up and seemed to come back to life. But it was just the memory of the seagull. The bird was already wheeling through the gray sky, and the willow was reduced to stone once more.

"Let's leave the past to the past . . ."

Those words came to me from various things I'd read long ago. We stayed there in silence until Antonio stood up abruptly.

"Come with me," he said. "I'm going to show you the Good Lord's tomb."

We left the restaurant, went back up toward Baixa, and headed into Elevador de Santa Justa. Only a few paces into the patchy shadows on that street Antonio opened the door to the Convento do Carmo, a ruin destroyed by the great earthquake. We stood among those white arches that gaped open like the ribcage of a whale skeleton. It had the feel of a cave without a roof, overrun with weeds, a dead place under the blue sky.

"So. Here we are."

He gestured toward the parched ground and broken stones.

"I used to play here for hours when I was a kid. Hunting lizards, destroying ants' nests, climbing the walls right up to the vaults: from up there you can see the whole lower part of the city. Later, Duck and I came here to kiss, at the foot of this very wall, with the wind blowing in from the sea making her hair fly in my face. No one bothered us, the tourists didn't care or didn't dare say anything, why would anyone mind a couple of youngsters having a good kiss . . ."

Antonio walked to the middle of the chapel, to the place where the altar must have been two centuries earlier, until beams and blocks of stone came crashing down onto the women and children who had hoped to find protection from their God's wrath in here.

"When I went to France I read Voltaire's poem about the Lisbon disaster. I even learned it by heart:

When you see all these victims will you say:
God is avenged, their lives for their crimes do pay?

For what crimes, what sins can children be found needing,
That now on their mothers' breasts lay crushed and bleeding?

"Yes, I knew it by heart. I sometimes think it was here in 1755, during the earthquake, that God died. And then four years ago . . ."

He stood in silence awhile, his expression vacant, then, without looking at me, he asked, "Do you know about the *carvoejadores* in Brazil?"

Yes, I knew about them. *Carvoejadores* meant people "cursed by charcoal." Children of six or seven gleaming with sweat and black with soot, working from dawn till after dark next to huge ovens burning eucalyptus wood. I had read an article about them years earlier. Antonio sat down on a block of stone, picked up a twig, and traced a circle in the dust.

"I did a photo-reportage for a German paper that paid well. It was on a large fazenda in Rondonia. They cleared several hectares of forest every day. I didn't have permission to be there, but I greased the guards' palms. The owners, the *fazendeiros*, made those kids work fifteen- or sixteen-hour days, for a couple of bowls of sugared cinnamon rice a day. Before having a barbecue, believe me, you should check where the charcoal comes from.

"I remember one tiny little boy, they called him Bombinha. That's the name they use for a *moleque da rua*, a little black street urchin. This Bombinha wasn't as smart as those kids usually are. He must have been very short-sighted, he bashed into everything, he fell down a lot and didn't recognize anyone unless they were close up, and even then he had to screw up his eyes. I don't know how he'd managed to survive, or how he'd ended up there, and he himself couldn't remember, it was as if fate had caught up with him and dropped him in that corner of hell. Fate, hell—just a pretty turn of phrase I used in the article. Recruiters used to kidnap those kids in the street, or just promise them food and somewhere to live. That was all it took."

He stopped talking, clenching and unclenching his fist as if lost in his own anger.

"Why am I telling you all this?"

"I'm not sure . . . You were talking about God, about God dying."

He gave a sad smile.

"Oh yes, the Good Lord . . . Bombinha got cut by a machete. On his leg. It wasn't deep, okay. He must have just sat on it without realizing. But the wound became infected, it was suppurating, it was a hideous sight. We cleaned it and covered it with moss, he clamped his teeth together with the pain, but didn't cry. But it kept getting worse. He got feverish, he was very sick. I started taking portraits of that kid, whole rolls of film, I don't know why, maybe because he was the same age as our child would have been, Duck's and mine, and while I took the pictures he would smile, he didn't think about the pain so much. I used to talk to him: Give me a nice smile, Bombinha, I know it hurts, but smile, I would say. I brought the photos back to Europe, the newspaper wanted to negotiate a price . . ."

Antonio was talking more and more quickly, his voice quavering. All around us, tourists in short-sleeved shirts were taking photos of the lacework of broken Roman arches, some of them laughing loudly.

"There was an American priest who kept an eye on them, a good sort who brought them food, and sandals too, I think his name was David. A Protestant preacher who'd left Kentucky behind, about fifty, I'm not sure. He looked older than that. David his name was, yes, that's right, David. Pretty symbolic, that name . . ."

He threw down the twig, picked up a little clod of earth and crushed it between his fingers. The soil fell to the ground in a fine dust, scattering ants beneath it.

"The guards didn't dare kill him, I'm sure that was because he had an American passport but also partly because he paid them. He wrote to the American consul in Rio every week, asking for their help. Actually, he sent letters all over the place, the poor man, he begged me to tell people what I'd seen there, and particularly not to forget it. I don't know where he lived, in some village, or a shack in the woods.

"When Bombinha was really ill the preacher came right away. He knelt down and prayed. Of course he knew medicine would have been more useful, just some antibiotics, but he'd run out, so there he was in that hut, holding the kid's hand, stroking his clammy hot forehead and reading him the Bible. I took a picture of that too, there was hardly any light, maximum aperture, but I had the shakes and the image was out of focus. But fuck, it was beautiful, I took some Fujicolors and some 400 ASAs, really pushing them, they looked like something by De La Tour, you know, his *Nativity*. They didn't want to run it in the paper. 'Your picture's out of focus,' they said, 'you can't see a thing.' What did the assholes want? For me to use a flash?"

Antonio was almost shouting. Tourists were giving us sideways glances, not quite daring to stare. Some were growing impatient, hovering around us, waiting for us to leave so they could get a photo of the whole convent.

"In the end they ran it with such a fucking dumb caption . . ."

Antonio took out a cigarette, which he didn't succeed in lighting because of the wind and because he couldn't get his fingers to work the lighter.

"In the end, the kid died, and when he did David was fast asleep beside him. Exhausted. He didn't see it happen. And I wasn't there either. When David woke and realized it was all over, he closed the boy's eyes and called me. I took the picture, afterward. Bombinha looks like he's sleeping in that shot, he looks restful. Really skinny, but restful. The other kids told us that just before he went, he whispered that he wanted his mother, he was delirious, asking for watermelon. David didn't say anything, he gave a few cruzeiros to the guards for permission to bury him himself, with all the kids there. He dug a little grave, planted a little cross, said a little prayer . . ."

Antonio stopped talking, his chin was wobbling, his eyes shining, and I stood there, not knowing what to do. One of the tourists gave a smile, made a gesture to ask us to move aside, to get a picture. Antonio stood up, then he just looked at the high white arches and said, "Come on . . . We're off."

IT MUST HAVE BEEN one o'clock in the morning, I was reading the paper to try and get to sleep. The world was full of Bombinhas. Full of photographers too, framing the vulture behind the dying little girl, because sometimes death can be photogenic. "There were hundreds of little girls like her," some guy from Gamma told me. "If we'd had to save her, we'd have ended up doing only that." Only: adverbial part of speech implying restriction.

I couldn't find it in me to feel sorry for him.

Someone once told me a good photographer had to take a pin with him. "Do you know why? To prick the baby in its mother's arms. Because a picture with the baby crying is always worth an extra ten dollars."

Who was it who told me that? Oh yes, Harry, that was one of Harry's stories. At the time I laughed so much, it was terrible, but perhaps Harry wasn't joking.

Harry was eighteen in 1944. He claimed to have been the youngest soldier at Omaha Beach, the youngest to come out of it alive, at least. He lied about his age to bring his call-up forward, so much so that when he reached Meaux in northern France he was barely nineteen and already a corporal. That may be a lie. With Harry, how do you know the truth from the lies? Either way, he got through dozens of rolls of film at Arromanches and Amiens, and in the Ardennes. He developed them at night, with developing fluid in GIs' helmets. In his New Jersey apartment he still had pictures of Patton at Malmédy, kneeling before the bodies of American prisoners machine-gunned down by the Germans. Those were the first photos he ever sold, in March 1945, to *Life*. The ones that made him famous.

I knew of another one, published around the same time. A simple grenade explosion near a bridge in Frankfurt. The picture was taken from very close quarters, it's a miracle he didn't leave his life there. It looks like a firework, for the Fourth of July. Except for an American soldier frozen in a peculiar, aerial motion, he was obviously already dead.

But there was one he had never wanted to have published. He always had a copy of it on him, protected with transparent adhesive film. On the back he had written:

"Munich, June 6, 1945." It was of a man of indeterminate age, wearing rags, his face appallingly thin, his eyes so sunken they could almost have been plucked out. He had no laces left in his shoes and he sat slumped amid the ruins. Before him, the dull gleam of a tiny piece of metal.

Perhaps he was a Jew who had survived one of the Polish death camps that the Soviets had liberated in January. Oświęcim. Later people said Auschwitz. Although Harry had not actually seen a single camp. Or only glimpses from a few photos published here and there in the papers, starting in April 1945 when the British entered Bergen-Belsen. The images were unbearable and yet Bergen-Belsen wasn't actually an extermination camp, hardly even one for the sick. Harry had cut them out, those photos, and—to keep his loathing for the Germans alive—he sometimes looked at the faces of those dazed, emaciated, spent clowns in their striped suits. That day in Munich was the first time he saw a deportee close up.

The man had mimed bringing food up to his twisted mouth, and had reached his hand out toward Harry. Then, when Harry didn't move, he clutched hold of him with his feeble skeletal fingers. He was filthy, covered in fleas and ringworm marks, stinking of putrefaction and piss. Harry looked away and pushed him off. To get rid of him, he rummaged through his pockets and threw him a dime. At the time, that wasn't too bad. The man reached clumsily for the coin but didn't manage to catch it. It rolled over the rubble. He ran to pick it up, but as he bent over he collapsed like an empty sack. Exhausted by the effort, he stayed there, gasping among the ruins. The coin gleamed a few centimeters from his hand, but he didn't have the strength left.

Harry had shuddered. It was not yet shame, just disgust. With himself, with the war, with that eye-popping stare fixed on the brass coin. Harry discovered he was capable of barbarity. He had crossed the invisible boundary that separates indifference from cruelty. A monster within him woke and proved stronger than the human being. It was getting dark. Harry walked away, not daring to look at the man who was still on the ground.

And yet, although he couldn't have said why, at the last minute he took the photo. The man, the coin, the ruins. The empty eyes.

An hour later, in the kitchen of a house requisitioned by his regiment, one of the few houses still standing in Munich, he developed the film and immediately made a set of prints. The picture came out in crisp focus, the framing was impeccable, it was the best of the roll. It was taken from just above the man, making him look truly alone, for all eternity, destitute. Only his hands were slightly out of focus, but that was probably because they had been shaking.

Harry put the picture down. He crouched on the ground and started shivering, and then whimpered like a wounded dog. Then he started punching the tiled floor, until blood oozed from his fingers.

Harry spent that night scouring the city, not really sure what he would do if he managed to find the man. By dawn he had interviewed dozens of people, old women, children, but in a bomb-ravaged Munich no one paid much attention to anyone else anymore. He sometimes said it was for the best, that his shame was now the truest part of him, that it had changed him permanently for the better.

Perhaps he was lying. Perhaps he was no better than before.

I put the newspaper down and turned out the light. I too had been a war correspondent for a while. The draw of the big wide world, the myth surrounding journalists, those words by the poet Supervielle about a pineapple-scented sadness worth more than a happiness that had never known travel. I too wanted to see the sun from another angle. One evening in 1981 when I was on the Mosquito Coast in the Sandinistas' Nicaragua, a .22 caliber bullet fired from a contra's M16 embedded itself in a beam less than two feet from my temple. It made the clean, powerful sound of an ax against a tree, and that pellet of steel gleamed in the half light. I flew back to Paris shortly after that and told the paper I was quitting, I was frightened; no one criticized me for it.

I was about to fall asleep when the telephone started ringing in Antonio's room, ringing and ringing. At first I thought he wasn't in there, that he had gone out in the night. But the ringing stopped and I heard his voice through the closed doors.

It was calmer than usual, very soft, and I guessed he was talking to a woman. It must have been a call from Paris, I only caught snatches of the conversation but it was in French. Sometimes his voice was a murmur like the whisper of a freshwater spring. I knew it was the woman he had mentioned, that she was unhappy, that he wouldn't find the words to comfort her.

So as not to listen, I concentrated on the *Contos aquosos* that I always kept close at hand. My copy was in good condition even though it was old, dated 1973. The cover was dog-eared, that was all.

Montestrela was obsessed with the passage of time, with old age, degeneration, and death. Half of the short stories tackled this theme, and not always with any distance, or even levity. Sometimes he also descended rather distressingly into pornography, even into scatological vulgarities not worthy of the lyrical poet who had once written the poignant *Prisão*, which Marguerite Yourcenar had praised for the "painful, almost martyred rhythm of its syllables." Still, I did not allow myself to censure anything, including stories such as this:

On the island of Pergos, under the reign of Toludey I, the law forbade anyone from taking anything without giving something at the same time. So the inhabitants drank only when they passed urine, and ate only when they defecated. Under these conditions, it was difficult to appreciate the aroma of the dishes during banquets, and culinary art in Pergos deteriorated until the Persian invasion in the third century B.C., an invasion that brought a salutary end to Toludeyan law.

At one point, I heard Antonio in his room almost shouting: "Don't cry, please, I beg you, don't cry . . ." There was the sharp clunk of him hanging up and almost immediately the sound of the telephone ringing again. This time Antonio picked up right away.

I switched on the bedside light and started scribbling the notes that helped me write this passage later. After a few minutes I heard footsteps in the lounge, the sound of a window being opened, and two very quiet knocks on my door.

I got out of bed and opened the door, Tonio was standing there holding two glasses. The lounge looked subtly alive in the half light, as if inhabited by the breeze and thrum of the city.

"Sorry to disturb you, I saw the light under the door. Did the phone wake you?"

I shook my head, but Tonio didn't wait for an answer and handed me a glass of beer.

"Here," he said. "I opened a couple of Sagres from the minibar. Nothing like a cold beer in the middle of the night . . ."

I smiled, reached my glass toward his, and he clinked them together with a shy, cautious expression that was probably appropriate for a new friendship. In the darkness his features looked unfamiliar, he looked handsomer, but older too, with more wrinkles and a more receding hairline. He could have been my brother.

"I'm really sorry about the phone. It was that girl, in Paris, the one who wrote the little note, you know."

He sighed, drank some beer. A thought seemed to come to him suddenly.

"Actually, I think you know her," he said. "It's Irene."

"Irene?"

"Yes. Such an old-fashioned name, isn't it?"

"Which Irene? The girl in archives? Small, with curly dark hair? Pretty?"

"Worse. You see, you do know her."

I don't know where I found the strength not to let anything show. I walked over toward the balcony and leaned against the stone parapet, my hands came to rest flat on the limestone surface, it was cold, rough, damp. My eyes misted over for a moment. I was afraid I would betray myself, afraid to know more too, but I asked, "Why did she call you?"

"Because she's in love with me. Or she thinks she is, which comes down to the same thing."

"Are you—together?"

"Yes, no, I don't know. We sleep together, that's all."

That's all. Two tiny words that described their mean-ingless lovemaking, their nights without tomorrows. And there was I who would have been able to love her so much more, so much better. A cold anger was growing inside me, a remote loathing, nothing violent, the sort you would feel for a torturer a long way away, one whose barbarity you only learned from the terrible accounts of his victims.

I thought of Galois's assassin, Pescheux d'Herbinville, and his murderous rage. It was not Stéphanie's lover he had challenged to a duel, it was the living reflection of his own powerlessness to be loved. Perhaps his jealousy had also revealed a hatred for Évariste that he had not previ-ously admitted to himself, a hatred for this unnecessar-ily brilliant adolescent whose intelligence and sheer life force eclipsed everything else, a hatred further fueled by the illusion of a long-standing friendship. I recognized that feeling of being nothing. It crushed me once again, this time thanks to this man and his instant and yet inex-plicable charm, this man who didn't even have to do any-thing to defeat me.

I kept a portrait of Galois on me, one of only a very few to have survived, an undated pencil drawing by an unknown artist. Galois's lips were thin and yet sensual, his nosed turned up at the end, his eyes bright and almost childlike. In that penciled image he could as easily be thirteen as twenty, even though it's not difficult to imagine he has the beginnings of a beard. The artist only had time to sketch his collar and the curve of his coat. Évariste must have posed for quite a while, before tiring. I often studied that face as if his incandescent gaze would somehow produce the words of my novel.

In the distance a man hailed a taxi in the dark. The car stopped and put on its hazard lights for a moment, and I thought that *Hazard Lights* would be a good title for this book or another, one day. The driver opened the door for the passenger and, with a squeal of tires, made a quick U-turn on the deserted Avenida da Liberdade. I watched the two red dots of his rear lights growing smaller, then fusing together and disappearing as the taxi turned right.

Antonio came to join me on the balcony, he looked down at the street and the square and brought his glass to his lips.

"I don't know what to do. Really."

He was waiting for a word from me, a sign of encouragement. On Restauradores Square a man and woman were kissing by the obscene yellow glow of streetlamps.

Antonio had no idea about our relationship. Otherwise, he would never have dared discuss Irene with me. Besides, I was sure she hadn't talked to anyone about me, sure I had never really existed as far as she was concerned.

Antonio's gaze roved over the city, alighting on every lurid neon sign, the red and electric blue of the Pasteleria Guzman, the red and yellow of the Splendid movie theater. He drank some more beer, the foam leaving a fold of white on his lips. For a moment I considered confessing everything to him. Telling him that because of her, every night, or almost, I left my room and walked aimlessly toward the river. Or I could throw my glass on the ground. But the least word, the least gesture would have sent me headlong into reality, and I did nothing, said nothing.

Antonio sighed and looked at my untouched beer.

"Aren't you drinking, don't you want it?"

I shook my head. A sense of calm settled. Over Irene and him. I didn't want answers to any questions.

A smile hovered over his lips. Which surprised me.

"You went out last night," he said. "I heard you."

"Yes."

"You've got someone here, haven't you? A woman? Your sleepless nights . . ."

He was smiling, and I smiled too because I was so surprised by his question. Antonio had invented a mistress for me, a woman to fill my thoughts.

"Yes . . . ," I replied, without thinking. And perhaps to tone down the lie, I added, "If you like."

"If I like?"

A lie. Quickly. Describe a woman, a meeting, strike the right note, watch the pauses, no hesitation about circumstances, places, times, no tripping up over words, or just the right amount. Talk about Irene too. Say enough for him to know, before he finds out, from her. I won a few seconds with a long draft of bitter beer.

"It's someone I met in Italy, three years ago, during that Mafia bombing in Parma, you remember. She's a painter . . . Well, she doesn't make a living from it, her real job is restoring works of art. Paintings. From the nineteenth century. She's Portuguese, she has a small apartment in Alfama, she spends two or three months a year there, in the summer. When I decided to come to Lisbon, I asked if I could rent it from her. She said that wouldn't be possible because she'd be there herself. When I arrived here she was at the airport waiting for me, and that was it."

I smiled again. So did Antonio.

"And what is this *bellissima signora* called?"

"L—Lena. Lena Palmer."

I was so unprepared for the question that I forged a stupid name, one so close to my own that I could anticipate Antonio's comment.

"Yes, I know, it's weird: I met a girl called Palmer in Parma and, worse, my name's Balmer, it's a sort of mirror image, and if I marry her she'll have a ridiculous name. But that's not her name, it's her husband's. Don't worry, her morals are safe, she's in the process of a divorce."

"Because of you . . ."

Go ahead, make fun of me, Antonio . . . Your sarcasm proved you were buying my story. I was sure you could already picture her, my Lena Palmer, far better than I could because I was busy trying to take on board each new lie. Lena Palmer. Actually, that Palmer was quite useful, there was no danger of forgetting it and giving myself away.

"Because of her husband, mostly because of him. A banker, or rather the financial director for a large industrial group, I never really grasped what he did. She married him, I don't know, ten years ago when she was just twenty and he was thirty-three, it couldn't work. Well . . . not because of the age difference, after all the man's nearly the same age as me. But twenty's too young to get married, wouldn't you say?"

"Whereas now . . . ," he ventured with a hearty laugh, baring his teeth.

"No, no, Antonio," I said with a smile. "Don't go imagining things. We haven't seen each other since Parma, you know . . . She's not sure what she wants with me, no more than I am . . . But you see, something happened, it was nothing really, but it makes me think this relationship could work: I didn't know she'd be at the airport, we'd agreed to meet a couple of hours later, at the Café Brasileira. In the crowds waiting at Arrivals, there was this really beautiful woman, unique in that mass of people, and my eyes were drawn to her, instant attraction. It was only a fraction of a second later that I recognized her as Lena, when she smiled at me and waved, delighted by my astonishment."

Antonio shook his head with a scornful laugh: "I don't know what you found so astonishing. You're lucky to think the woman you love is pretty."

"I don't know how to explain it, I really don't. She didn't even have to be pretty . . ."

Even though I had created my Lena, I didn't feel like sharing any intimate details with Antonio, who didn't understand. I didn't mean physical attraction, or that possessive vanity that takes hold of some men who are proud of their partner's good looks. I wanted to pinpoint the moment just after that instant, unfounded attraction, the fraction of time when anonymous desire gives way to specific tenderness, when the attraction of a face is replaced by the sweet pleasure of memories.

I paused for a while, pretended to drink my beer, but the glass was empty.

"And then nearly two months ago, I fell in love with someone else, so . . ."

"Do you want another Sagres?" Antonio asked.

Don't interrupt me, Antonio, please, because this is where the real lie begins. I'm going to tell you about Irene, about her and me. Hiding feelings is so much harder than inventing new ones. I smiled and shook my head.

"No thanks, no more beer. The woman I was in love with, you'll never guess . . . it was Irene."

Just saying her name was painful.

"Irene?"

Antonio looked genuinely amazed. I had guessed right, Irene hadn't said a thing.

"Yes . . . Oh, it wasn't very serious. Anyway, there's nothing between us now."

"I don't understand . . ."

"We had dinner together, quite often, we even went away together, but she was always distant. Seriously distant in fact."

I laughed. A bright, cheerful laugh, truly.

"I don't think she knew what she wanted. And I must have been really, really heavy. An analyst would have said I was developing a fixation. I should probably have gone out and got myself a goldfish or a cat."

I burst out laughing stupidly, and thought to myself that Irene most likely cared more for her cat than for me. What was his name again? More of a dog's name, I think. Pluto, Plato?

"Is she the reason you left Paris?"

"No. This trip was planned a long time ago . . . Three or four months."

Antonio looked concerned, far more than I would have suspected. I panicked slightly. My confession was meant to protect me, and I suddenly realized that my desire for Irene might rekindle his own feelings for her. Worse, it could fan the flames of those feelings, give them a whole new meaning.

"And do you still think about her?"

There was a pressing, almost anxious note in his voice. I needed to reassure him, take a step back, stop being a threat.

"No. Sometimes, a bit. But it doesn't hurt, I'm just amazed to have misread things so badly. And anyway, there's Lena . . ."

I looked at my watch, a quasi-instinctive gesture, discreet but almost impatient, to make Antonio assume I was supposed to be meeting Lena. I said a bit more about this woman, the amber of her eyes, such a rare color, the smell of her. I think I was plausible.

Antonio let me talk, and when I ran out of empty sentences, a sad-looking smile flitted across his face.

"You and Irene . . . I didn't know, I would never have imagined . . ."

He gave a small private laugh, little more than a breath, and it hurt me.

Why would you never have imagined, Antonio? Was there something absurd, ridiculous about her and me? Yes, of course, you're right. What with her being so young next to my forty years, my thinning hair, my deepening wrinkles, my body which wants to pass itself off as smooth and firm but isn't very convincing anymore. What was it Irene once said? Oh yes, it was a young man's body that hadn't aged well. It was a cruel turn of phrase, and a pointless one too, because surely she knew no one ever ages well.

"Do you know why I'm laughing?" he asked. "I wanted to ask you to help me. To help me write to her."

"Write to her? About what?"

"I don't know, to say I love her, or I don't love her yet . . . to tell her . . . about how confused my feelings are. I write so badly, I'm so awkward. I don't want to hurt her. You'd have been better at finding the words than me. I honestly thought you didn't know her. Well, not like that. I read a short story you once wrote for the paper. For you it would have been . . ."

I put down my glass, afraid Antonio would notice my hand shaking. And I finished his sentence: ". . . just an exercise in style . . . a little Cyrano de Bergerac moment. Minus the nose, I might say."

"Yes, if you like . . . Let's drop the subject."

I had the seeds of an idea which made me smile. A bitter smile, but in the darkness Antonio could have read it as friendly.

"No, it's okay, Antonio, I understand. It doesn't bother me, not at all . . ." My eyes didn't betray a thing, I'm sure they didn't betray a thing. "Let's write this letter."

I laughed and asked for another Sagres. Antonio would be reassured seeing me pouring it carefully into the glass, eyeing the froth in eager anticipation, then bringing it to my lips. I performed this little beer-lover routine, nicely underplaying it. A man so focused on slaking his thirst is not one who's suffering. And in spite of myself, I appreciated that beer, it was nice and cool, with a tangible, noticeable bitterness. I felt freer, more alive.

"Does Irene know I'm in Lisbon?" I asked. "That I'm working with you?"

"I've no idea. I don't think so."

"You need to tell her. She'll find out sooner or later. And then . . ." I tried to find the words as I stroked the rough stone of the balcony.

"Also, tell her you know about her and me. That I mentioned it. You see, let's be honest, we parted in difficult circumstances. I was quite . . . nasty—a bit of an asshole to be frank. That's ancient history, but I don't want her thinking I would try to keep you two apart, out of jealousy or revenge. Do you see what I mean?"

"Yes . . . of course."

I drank some more beer, tried to think of other lines of argument.

"She cares about you, that's obvious. And when you care about someone, you worry about everything . . ."

Antonio nodded in silence. I moved my last pawn into position: "No more hesitating . . . I think we should even admit to her about Lena and me."

I was very pleased with myself for finding that "we," making us accomplices. I mustn't abuse that complicity, whatever happened. Men struggle with the notion of "we," or rather when they have a "we" it often ends badly, in dubious conniving. I finished my beer and put the glass down resolutely: "I'm sure she'll find it reassuring knowing I'm in love with someone else . . ."

I looked at my watch again, automatically. It was one o'clock in the morning. I got ready to leave even though it was far from plausible to be meeting anyone so late.

Antonio smiled. "Is this Lena of yours a night owl?"

"She sometimes paints right through the night, using artificial light. If the light's on in her window, I'll know."

He opened the fridge and took out another bottle.

"I'm going to stay here for a bit, Vincent, it'll give me a chance to think . . . so, how about tomorrow?"

"Tomorrow? What tomorrow?"

"The letter . . . can we write it tomorrow?"

He took the top off the bottle, some froth spilled over his fingers, obscenely.

"Yes, that's right," I replied, "we'll write it tomorrow."

I LEFT THE HOTEL and tried to find a taxi. At exactly the same time, Antonio was calling Irene, she was talking to him tenderly. I walked a few paces, if that, my head spinning. I leaned against the wall and slid down onto my heels, my legs buckling beneath me. I stayed there for many minutes before going home to my studio. I put an album on the deck, Sting's *The Dream of the Blue Turtles*, which I had bought the day I broke up with Irene, and I lay down on the bed to listen to "If You Love Somebody Set Them Free" on a loop.

It was that night I made my decision. I would put up one last fight, with all the fire and skill typical of serial losers, of people who have gone from one defeat to the next so often that winning no longer means anything to them. The hopeless philosophy of the old, the ugly, and the poor.

I was going to search for Duck, and was going to find her. At some point predetermined by me, Antonio would meet her and I would find a way of rebuilding their lost happiness, I would rewrite fate, I would be their fate. I wanted Irene to come, to be there, in Lisbon so that she could see her ruin; and the city that had brought Tonio and Duck together would be my most faithful ally.

That would be my complete revenge, that wound to her pride, the pain she would feel. I knew I no longer wanted Irene, I would be able to reject her, to say with a smile but without hatred that she meant nothing to me now, and never would again.

But almost immediately, despite my own plans, I also hoped that in that confusion of passions, that muddle of emotions, she would finally conceive some feeling for me. Something unclear at first, but that might one day be like love.

What did Montestrela say about love? "When you're making it, don't think about the fact that at that very moment, someone, somewhere, is dying."

DAY THREE

■

*A*URORA

hen I returned to the hotel Antonio was still asleep. His jacket was lying on one of the armchairs. I stood there in the silence for a moment. I pulled his wallet from the pocket and took out the photo of Duck. Just a loan, for no more than a few hours, time enough to make a copy.

There was another picture, this one in black and white. Antonio was in it, looking very young, in a group of other young men. It was almost like a class photo. I didn't want to spend too long studying it. I took it as well. For no reason.

Then I went to bed and fell straight into a deep sleep. Antonio told me later that I snored, and I grimaced my apology. I hate those periods of complete abandon, a languor in which I can picture my flaccid, noisy hideousness, my face on the pillow like a dead jellyfish, my mouth half open, my breath fetid, times when—yet again—I wish I were someone else.

THAT MORNING THE press announced that the Pinheiro trial would begin any day, and I bought every newspaper. Leader writers had reopened their files, reused the photographs of bloodied corpses, recapped the circumstances of each murder. Soon the victims' families would be put through it all again.

When Pinheiro was arrested, I had written two or three columns about the man they were calling the Mad Killer of Lisbon. They had chosen a photograph of him as a young man with a laughing face and a sailor's uniform, accompanied by an enticing caption.

When he turned fifty, he changed into a small, thin man with brown hair, a smooth face, and sad, nearly gray eyes. A man with no history, virtually invisible. At the time of his arrest, he had been working as an administrator in the port's customs offices for more than ten years. An honest, scrupulous employee, well viewed by his superiors, liked by his co-workers, a bachelor not known to have any relationships, no enemies, nor friends in fact. If he ate out in the evening, it was always alone, and when he had lunch in the customs canteen, he took a book from his leather case and never joined in conversations.

Antonio had called the hospital where Pinheiro was incarcerated, and had had little trouble securing an interview with the psychiatric expert. We were to meet him in three days.

IT WAS STILL early when we went down to the port and along to berth 24, drawn by a sound of tortured steel. In berth 13, I noted in my notebook, an old cargo boat with a Russian flag was baring its prow with a fresh three-foot scar in it. A workman balancing on a hanging footbridge was cutting away the dented sheet metal with a circular saw. Sprays of red sparks swirled around him, accompanied by a strong smell of burning and an almost unbearably strident noise. Under his heavy welding mask and thick leather overalls, the man handled the machine powerfully and with such ease that he seemed extraordinarily strong.

Antonio started taking pictures at machine gun speed with his Leica, then thrust the camera at me rather violently.

The telephoto lens shielded the view from the sky's brilliance, making the scene both more immediate and more terrifying. Against a background of rust and sickening metal, the workman had pride of place among waterfalls of fire, the blacksmith god of lava and volcanoes. I released the shutter, heard its crisp click and the soft whirr of the motor.

I turned slowly and Antonio appeared in the black rectangle. Small red numerals lined up in the viewfinder, right in the middle of his chest. He was standing in profile, his features distorted by the bluish shade of the filthy cargo boat that filled the picture beside him. Coils of rope lay behind him, like sleeping black pythons. Farther away, a giant crane stood out in the sunlight, truncated sharply by the corner of the shot. I took the picture, not sure whether the light levels were good enough.

Antonio came over to me slowly, pointing toward me. His cheek was colored by the electric glow of the sparks, and the wail of the saw drowned out everything. There was something strange or even aggressive about the gesture he was making, and I saw it as a threat, a trap. What did Antonio want from me that I was so afraid of losing, that I hadn't already lost? I took a step back, penetrated by the chill that precedes a ghostly apparition, panicked by my incomprehensible terror.

Time stretched out and slowed down as it had in childhood nightmares where I was pursued by monsters, where my hopeless stumbling flight got me nowhere, where the vampires and dinosaurs always inevitably caught up with me. Antonio was coming closer, he was smiling, an enemy's smile. All at once his giant hand hid his face from me. Then his palm covered the lens and everything went red and black.

I staggered. Antonio looked at me, concerned.

"Are you all right, Vincent? You look pale . . ."

"I need to sit down a minute, I must be overtired. I—I'm not sleeping much at the moment."

Antonio laughed, winked, gave me a little pat on the shoulder. The friendly physical contact made me shudder.

"I'm feeling better. Let's go back."

"No, no, let's wait for a bit. There, look, how about going over there?"

He was pointing to a large barge with sky-blue sides, a cable's length from the quay but connected to it by a long narrow footbridge. A bistro terrace had been set up on its deck, with wobbling garden tables, Fanta parasols in faded colors, and, stranded in the middle, a sort of prefabricated yellow workman's hut. On the quay, an oval sign with rounded blue letters announced STROMBOLI'S, ITALIAN SPECIALTIES.

We were just boarding the barge when a good-natured, bald imp in a white apron sprang from the hut.

"We're closed, the restaurant's closed!" The little man ran over to us and stood puffing at the end of the footbridge. "It's José, he didn't take the sign down, so you obviously have no way of knowing, but we're closed—I can't let you—"

"Be kind," said Antonio, "my friend's feeling faint."

"Faint? Oh . . ." The fellow moved aside, as if I were contagious. "Well, you *are* white as a sheet. You must be having an attack of hippopotitis . . . Don't move a muscle, okay? I'll be back . . ."

While Antonio stifled his explosive laughter, the man pushed a white plastic chair toward me, dusting it carefully: "Sit yourself there, sir . . . There you are . . . I'll bring you something to drink. A glass of water, or no, better than that, a Coke, it's stuffed full of sugar, it'll clear your head and do you good."

Before I had a chance to refuse he was running for his hideout. The blood pounding in my temples was already calmer. I heard the sound of a car door and looked over to the quay.

A woman was sitting at the wheel of a little red Fiat, beside a large container. She took one last energetic drag on her cigarette and threw the stub out the window. The sun must have been in her eyes, she looked away, turned the key in the ignition, and drove off. I had seen her face for only a second. From that distance she looked like Duck. If that's who it was, she hadn't seen Antonio, and because he was sitting facing the sun, he couldn't have seen her. I stood up, the car was already driving away. Antonio also turned, too late. The Fiat had disappeared behind a warehouse.

"What is it, Vincent? You're still very pale."

"I—I thought I recognized someone . . ."

"Your Lena Palmer? You see her everywhere . . . not a good sign. You've got it bad."

I shook my head.

"No, it's nothing. I must have been wrong . . ."

Our enthusiastic imp was back already with a bottle and a kindly smile. He uncapped it and handed it to me.

"Here, drink that," he said and winked as he added, "it's the real thing, you know, I make it myself."

He stood up and found two more chairs for Antonio and himself. Then he suddenly looked worried.

"Hey, are you sure you don't want to call a doctor?"

"No thanks, I'm feeling better already."

"All right. Well, that's a relief, because I do have a phone here, but it's out of order."

He watched me for a moment, suspiciously, while I drank the sparkling too sugary drink and he ran his hand over his sweating head.

"If you want my opinion, it's because of the heat. You don't really notice, but it's very hot already, isn't it?"

Antonio nodded in silence. "Are you Italian?" he asked, pointing at the sign.

"No, I'm from Porto, like my father. But my mother, now *she*'s from Milezza in Sicily. That's why I called the restaurant Stromboli's. And I have an Italian name too. Leopoldo. Well, Leo. But I thought Stromboli's sounded better than Leo's. Don't you think?"

There was a warm westerly breeze heavy with salt blowing off the sea.

"There's *always* a bit of wind in this part of the port. It even carried off one of my parasols once."

I don't know whether I owed it to Leopoldo's remedy, but I was feeling better. I took a step toward the footbridge, reached for my wallet.

"You must be joking!" the little man said indignantly, shaking our hands. "But you have to come and eat here, you will, won't you? I'll make *penne all'arrabiata* for you. It's the house specialty, lots of chili, lots of garlic, lots of olive oil. And two or three pieces of penne, well, you have to. So, do you promise?"

We promised and left the barge. I would have liked to follow the route taken by the Fiat, perhaps it wasn't that far away, but Antonio insisted on heading toward the streets he had known as a child.

We climbed up a narrow street toward Bairro Alto.

"You see there, Vincent, where there's an electrical store, there used to be a hardware store, maybe it's the old owner's son who's now selling Walkmans. He always used to hang things outside, dish racks and plastic bowls in sky blue, bright yellow, every color. When he opened in the morning he hung bunches of them from the awning, like Chinese lanterns. The candy was kept inside in glass jars, with lids to stop thieving fingers. He had hard candy, caramel, red and green barley sugar . . ."

"Did you come here with Duck?"

"I don't remember. When I was with her I didn't feel much like eating candy."

"Where did she live?"

He tilted his chin toward one of the ten-story buildings at the top of the street. It was built in the sixties and had about a hundred peeling balconies, all laden with parched potted plants, broken old toys, bicycles, and laundry dryers.

"Do you remember which apartment it was?"

"No, just that it was on the other side of the building. On the seventh or eighth floor, I can't remember. From her bedroom you could see the April 25 Bridge and the statue of Christ the King."

Antonio looked away and we slowed imperceptibly.

We walked toward Eduardo VII Park, toward the clammy heat of Estufa Fria. Antonio couldn't wait to rediscover the smell of the tropical hothouses, and he bought two tickets.

A slatted wooden canopy softened the sun's rays. We wandered among the ferns and umbrella trees, and followed the meanders of an artificial river that snaked through the gardens. Antonio stopped from time to time to take a photograph.

A tousled-haired kid in sandals ran up to Antonio. He was holding a long cluster of milk-white flowers.

"Here," he said, handing him the flowers with his arm held high. It was an insistent, determined gesture, not the sort of childish command that could be shrugged off. Antonio knelt, accepted the present, and put it in his buttonhole.

"Like that?" he asked.

"Yes, that's great like that."

The boy backed away slightly to look at Antonio and said solemnly, "They'll bring you good luck. What are you going to give me in exchange?"

Antonio reached up and took his wallet from his jacket. I blenched: I hadn't yet had time to put back the two photos after having them copied. All Antonio offered was a stamp, a French one.

"Here, it's a French stamp. Is that okay?"

"That's robbery . . . ," the kid retorted sulkily. He rubbed his head to show he was thinking, and added, "But it'll do. Just this once."

And he put the stamp in his pocket.

An elderly man appeared behind the child, slightly out of breath. He was holding his hat in his hand and automatically raised it above his head to greet us.

"Oh dear, oh dear, oh dear! Please forgive him, he does whatever he pleases. Marco, did you pick that off a tree? You mustn't take flowers off the trees. Oh, I can't cope with him, he won't stay still for a moment."

The child had already gone on ahead, escaping his minder.

"Marco, wait for me. Do forgive him, really, please."

The old man trotted off in pursuit of the boy, and Antonio put the viewfinder to his eye, snapping the pair of them before they disappeared behind the foliage.

We crossed a bridge sculpted out of cement, then another. Passing by waterfalls and lagoons, the path took us to an indoor pond covered in water hyacinths. In the middle of this small lake stood a gray-and-pink marble building, it was imposing, monumental even, and overrun with creepers. It must have been the hothouse curator's home or a reception area for summer shows. We were alone on the edge of the water, and I felt uncomfortable. We shouldn't have been there, we had gone into an area out of bounds to visitors.

On the paved terrace in front of the building, sitting between the paws of a marble lion, a girl was twisting and turning a bamboo stick in the water. At first I thought she couldn't have been more than sixteen. She was wearing a short dress with a red-and-blue pattern, her legs were slender but toned and tanned, and her black hair was held in a multicolored ribbon. Beside her on the flat tiles lay a sketchbook covered with pictures in charcoal and pastels. An old case for a child's violin lay open, full of oil pastels. She didn't appear to notice us and, for a moment, perhaps because she looked so unaware and peaceful, the place seemed to belong to her for all eternity.

She was describing shapes in the emerald water, ephemeral figures, no two the same, manipulating the bamboo

precisely, unhesitatingly. It was as if she was forming letters, writing words long forgotten by the waters but carried to us silently on the shimmering wavelets.

Antonio was mesmerized. He set off along a paved path
that ran through the water lilies and other water plants,
crossing the lake that lay between us and the terrace.
Something about the way he moved made me think he
knew her, but he asked, "What's your name?"

Antonio's presumptuous familiarity, his intrusion, wasn't
paternal, it didn't have the authority of an adult addressing
an adolescent. It had more to do with an instant instinctive
intimacy, the first words from a besotted prince to a shep-
herdess, or rather a fascinated shepherd to a princess.

"Aurora," she replied, not looking up or even stopping
her twirling of the bamboo in the lagoon.

All at once she threw the stick in the water and stared
at Antonio and then at me, as I too crossed toward the
terrace, clumsily, trying not to slip on the mossy paving
stones. She jumped to her feet and when she looked me in
the eye I realized she reminded me of Irene, because of her
black, almond-shaped eyes, olive skin, and other indefin-
able qualities.

"Are you two lost? You realize this is my house, here,
my island?"

Antonio smiled. "Your island?"

"Yes. It may not actually be completely an island but it is
mine. I come here whenever I like, even when it's closed. I

have the keys to the little door at the end. That's where my father keeps his machines. I always do my studying here. Textile drawings, but not printed patterns. I mean I do designs for woven fabrics. Do you know what I mean? Look."

She opened her sketchbook at random. Every inch of paper was covered with sketches of geometric designs. One area looked like the cubist weave of cotton, another like pencil-drawn stitches in wool.

She stood on tiptoe and smelled the flowers on Antonio's lapel.

"That's pretty. *Clivia minata.* And where was it stolen?"

"Some kid just gave it to me," Antonio apologized, embarrassed. "It's a good luck charm . . ."

"Really? A good luck charm? Do you believe in good luck, then?"

She pirouetted on the spot.

"At night I sometimes light the little blue suns," she said, pointing to ultraviolet lights on the roof arches.

"At night?" Antonio asked, smiling and running his hand through his red hair in a rather contrived, affected way.

The girl crouched, closed her sketchbook, and started clearing the pastels scattered over the paving stones into the violin case.

"Don't you believe me? Are you laughing at me?"

"No, I didn't mean to hurt you."

She looked down, arranging her oil pastels in order like the colors of the rainbow. Antonio knelt beside her, picked

up a few crayons, and handed them to her. Without looking up, she took them and said, "And do you two have
names? You, what's your name?"

"Antonio, Antonio Flores. And my friend is Vincent.
Vincent Balmer."

I introduced myself with a bow.

"Vincent Balmer? Are you English, then?" Aurora
asked, but not waiting for a reply, she turned to Antonio: "And what about Flores? Is that really your name? Is
that why you've come to see your cousins the flowers?
That's Jewish, isn't it? They say all flower and tree names
are Jewish. My name's Jewish too, it's Oliveira. And my
middle name's Judith. But I was baptized. Gods are so
complicated."

Of all the pastels she chose cyan and ran it along her
forearm, tracing a streak of azure, like war paint.

"I'll draw a bird for you Antonio, okay?"

She snatched Antonio's wrist like a bird of prey launching itself at a mouse. In one fluid movement she drew a
beak and a neck on his palm, created the line of a wing
on his thumb, then another on his little finger, and, on his
index finger, a long tail like a magpie's, pointing upward.
She put down the blue crayon, picked up a sunny yellow
one, and, with a roll of her fingers, created the eye in
the middle of his palm where his heart line and luck line
crossed. She let go of Antonio's hand and put away the
pastels.

"Bird-hand, by Aurora Oliveira," she laughed. "A good luck charm, and this one's real. A bird in the hand is worth two in the bush, you know."

Antonio moved his hand and the bird came fleetingly to life, spreading its wings, ready to fly. Antonio opened and closed his hand slowly, fascinated, unable to say a thing, and Aurora watched him closely, smiling. In the golden light, Antonio's hair looked almost brown, and for the second time I thought him handsome, even more so. Then he turned to Aurora, and his whole voice had changed, husky but gentle too: "How old are you, Aurora?"

"Twelve." Antonio opened his eyes wide and she burst out laughing: "No, I'm not, I'm thirty. What about you? Don't say a thing, don't tell me, whatever you do, you fool . . . Telling your age makes you older."

A sudden bright light made me look up. Something was twinkling far overhead, way up in a huge rubber palm whose leaves hung over the top of the building, over the bay window. The twinkling came from a pair of round, steel-framed glasses. As it had grown, the plant had gradually engulfed the metal sidepieces, and the glasses were set right into the trunk. Two growths within the wood, two bulging green protuberances, formed a pair of frog-like eyes. I instinctively pushed my own glasses back up my nose. Aurora noticed the gesture.

"Are you admiring Monstro?" she asked. "When I was little, even littler, it used to frighten me with its strange cut-out leaves, like witches' masks. So I put an old pair of glasses between two of its branches. Then when it grew they were imprisoned. I called it Monstro because, according to the gardeners, it's a *monstera deliciosa*. And it was the name of the whale in *Pinocchio*, you know, the film of *Pinocchio* . . ."

I couldn't take my eyes off Monstro, off that pair of glasses trapped in the thick trunk where acrid white sap must have been seeping over them. That fragment of human life gave the towering plant a strange personality. Behind the filthy lenses, you could almost imagine there lurked a climbing-plant philosophy, with sententious words impounded in its chlorophyll.

Aurora was smiling mischievously. She must have been keeping a real, far deeper secret.

"Well," said Antonio, "I think Monstro was one of your lovers and you were bored of him and turned him into a philodendron."

Aurora touched Antonio's cheek very lightly.

"You're so clever, Antonio," she said mockingly. "You guessed. I always turn my lovers into plants, do you think there would be this many here otherwise? Over there, that drooping fatsia, the one that needs water and is drying out because I won't let anyone water it, that's that idiot José. He was always hovering around me, constantly trying to look at my breasts, when he gave me an ice cream, when he read a book over my shoulder . . . One day, what a nightmare, he put his hand on my hip. Ugh, it was disgusting. And in a flash, changed him into a fatsia. Ciao, José."

She ran over to a burgeoning plant clinging to a wall of rock.

"This staghorn fern here is Ruiz, he always wanted people to believe he was a real man. He rolled his pack of cigarettes in the sleeve of his T-shirt and made a lot of noise on his scooter. He's much quieter like this, with these dangling fronds like dogs' tongues."

She gave a sneer to staghorn-Ruiz, walked on a few paces, and stroked a leaf on a palm tree near the water lilies.

"And this howea which won't stop growing is Tadeus. He was the kindest one. He used to say, 'Tell me, Aurora, do you think you'll ever love me? Because, as you know, I just adore you and I want to live with you.' He was so sweet, poor Tadeus . . . Then he got a bit too persistent and eventually even quite nasty. There's no getting away from it, with boys, if they love you and you don't love them they call you a bitch. That's oversimplifying, isn't it?"

Aurora talked on and on with an almost singsong accent, and I could see Antonio was increasingly unsettled.

"Monstro's another story," Aurora went on, "I don't like shortsighted boys. They make you feel you should protect them, and when they wake up in the morning their glasses are always more important than you. One day Monstro—"

I put my hand up to my glasses without even thinking, and she burst out laughing. She tapped her finger on the copy of *Contos aquosos* that was peeping out of my pocket.

"What are you reading?"

"They're short stories."

I handed the book to her, and she took it and leafed through it, frowning, but smiling too.

"Jaime Montestrela . . . What a weird name. It doesn't mean anything to me. The stories are weird too."

She handed it back to me, made as if to leave the terrace along the paved path, but turned back, rummaged through her large canvas bag, and took out two invitation cards which she slipped into Antonio's hand.

"I almost forgot: you must come tomorrow, there's a concert. Baroque music, Purcell, Monteverdi, you'll see when you get here. It's at eight o'clock sharp, on the nose, you need to wear a suit, it says so on the invitation. I'll be wearing a full-length dress. You'll see there are plenty of people who'll want to get their tuxedos out, and it looks very funny in the hothouse, like a colony of penguins visiting the Amazon. Okay, see you tomorrow then?"

She ran off, a gazelle, and vanished into her jungle. I heard the motor of Antonio's Leica. She was already hidden but her voice echoed round the hothouse: "Come back soon, Antonio, and I'll draw a cat for you on your other hand."

"NO, ANTONIO, NOT like that . . . Don't say *My Irene*,
don't start with that possessive, it's too worn, too over-
used, just say *Irene*, it's truer, stronger, more sensitive.
She'll read her name and hear your voice saying it, you
breathing it, and *Irene*'s a word that never really ends, it
hangs in the air long after you've said it, it doesn't need
anything else.

"Write: *Irene, I'm lost, I don't know what I want.* After all,
that's always true, we never have any idea what we want
from other people. *When I left for Lisbon*—no, you weren't
leaving, it was a separation, a wrench, so write *When I set
off from Paris*, yes, that's better, it's much better to refer
to the place you're leaving than some nebulous destina-
tion. *When I set off from Paris, I couldn't know that you would
become*—no, actually, *that I had become such an important
part of your life. I don't like thinking you're hurt, I didn't want
either of us to be hurt.*

"This letter needs to be short, it's better to show you
don't feel comfortable with words, so start a new paragraph, pause, let your writing catch its breath: *Irene, dear
sweet Irene*—but did you ever call her sweet? You didn't?
Well, do it then, it'll be like you're daring to use words in
this letter that you held back in person, words you've never
spoken, that will be hers all brand-new and subtly different.

"Look out the window, Antonio, let the city speak for you. Tell her it's two in the morning, or even later, it's raining in Lisbon, and I can see the Avenida da Liberdade from the window, it's glistening and gloomy as a canal in Amsterdam. That's a bit of a hollow image, Antonio, I realize, but have a look, don't you think that tonight Lisbon looks like a cold northern city, silent in the mist, and that the deserted street's reflecting the darkness the way a slow-moving waterway would? And you need to give this letter a bit of color, even if it is gray, particularly if it's gray. Say *I want to sleep, but I can't, the sound of the rain, perhaps, or a feeling that I'm not getting anywhere with my work, or my life. I shot two or three rolls of film today, in the port. I don't know what they're going to be like, these articles I'm working on with Vincent. We have ten days left to wrap everything up, and I feel I don't recognize this place, even though not much has changed in ten years.*

"Then say, *Of course, I didn't tell you Vincent Balmer's in Lisbon with me.* There, Antonio, that's when she needs to find out. Make the point *He lives here now. As of two months ago. Or a bit longer. A big room in the port neighborhood. Not very tidy. Anyway, we took rooms in a hotel together. It's more practical.* Explain that *He's doing the writing. He spends his days making notes, in the big black book he takes everywhere with him, and he speaks Portuguese with a funny accent, like he's imitating a Portuguese imitating a Frenchman imitating a Portuguese, or the other way around.* Does that make you laugh, Antonio?

But it's true, isn't it? Write it. *He's not very chatty but the two of us get on well.* We can say that, Antonio, can't we? Don't say anything more. If you say too much, it'll never be enough. She'll want to have details, to work out how much you know, to try and read between the lines.

"*The hotel's comfortable, a bit impersonal, but I think it suits our work.* I know, Antonio, here you can add in this, it's a snippet from my notes, it fits perfectly with your last sentence: *The place is both tired-looking and luxurious, dating back to the early 1900s, one of those palaces where you never feel at home, and never even want to unpack your bags.* Say *Irene, what if you came and joined me?* No, that's a stupid, bland construction with that simpering *what if* like a childish game. Say *Come and join me in Lisbon.* And don't look at me like that, Antonio, I'm sure it's a good idea. You'll be on your territory here, everything will seem clearer. Don't worry about me, I'll go and sleep in my studio in São Paulo. Or with Lena. I'll leave you in peace. You can give yourself enough time to be sure. Say *For a few days at least. A long weekend.*

"We need to finish this letter, make it short. No lying now, we can't go and end it with a stock phrase, an *I miss you* or an *I can't stop thinking about you.* Anyway, you're not in love yet, she'd know you were lying. Girls can see through everything, they're so clever. Just say *I'd really like to show you the city where I grew up. You take good care of yourself*—no, put *really good care.*

"And sign it. Legibly. Not impatiently. As if you regret it.

"Shall we tell her about Aurora, in a PS? No, come on, Antonio, I'm kidding. I'm kidding, I tell you."

"SHE USED TO LIVE in this building, you say?"

The man filled the whole doorway, his arms were huge, larded with unhealthy fat. On his wrist he wore a heavy gold watch, and a chain, also gold, hung over his flaccid white chest. It wasn't all that hot, but he was sweating, and sweat flecked his shirt.

He was holding the duplicate picture of Duck between his fingers, and I had an urge to take it back from him, as if he might soil it. His obese figure made me feel uncomfortable, like a reflection of my own ugly intentions. I nearly capitulated and turned back for the hotel.

"Yes, that's right, she lived in this building. On this side, actually. It's just the floor I'm not sure about."

"Ten years ago, you say? Wait . . ." And without turning around he cried, "Baby? Ba-by?"

It made me jump. A woman appeared behind him. Small, thin, dark-haired, in her fifties, a hard face with black eyes, not unlike a witch.

"Look at this, Baby, do you recognize her? This man says she lived here."

He rubbed his hand over his sweating face.

"I work nights, so, you know, people from the building . . ."

The woman wiped her hands on her apron and studied the photograph for a long time, and then me for even longer. The man stepped aside to let her through and disappeared into the apartment without a word. She took the picture and turned it over as if looking for a date or a note.

"What do you want from this girl?"

"I'm looking for her . . . it has to do with a legacy. All I know is she lived here, in this building."

"A legacy . . . But tell me, this picture was taken a long time ago." It was not a question, and there was a harsh note of reproach in her voice. "At least five years, isn't it?"

"Ten years."

I said this quietly, as if asking forgiveness for the passing years, and she looked back at the photo, her eyes more human now.

"You're French, aren't you, you have an accent, " she said, her voice softer. "A legacy, you say? Who's died? She didn't have any family in France, poor little thing—"

"So you do know her?"

The woman sighed.

"Of course I know her," she said, "like everyone in the building, well, the ones who were here at the time. Because there's a lot of coming and going in the neighborhood, it's getting expensive for the likes of us, the rents are going up so much."

She peered up at me.

"Now, this girl, yes, I remember her, she had a funny name, something like Arnica, or Arcana, but everyone called her something else."

"Arcana?"

The voice grew suspicious: "But you must know the girl's name if you're really looking for her."

"No, I don't have a name like that . . . I have one or two clues, and this photo. I've been paid to find her, that's all. You see, she's inheriting from an American, not someone in her family, but you know, the will is impeccably within the law, even if I don't have a name. Under U.S. law, well, Texas state law, you can leave your pet canary to someone if you want."

"Texas . . ."

The word came to me just like that, but it had its effect. The woman looked convinced, because she shook her head.

"No, I don't know where she is. She got pregnant, she wasn't even fifteen, and her father sent her away north, I think. He moved away after that. A real bastard."

She took a step back, I thought she was going to walk away so I persisted: "You really have no idea where I should try to look for her?"

"No. You could always go asking at the tasca, on the rua das Tangentes. Ask if anyone's heard from Ruiz, yes, that was her father's first name, he sometimes has a drink there with the regulars. Ask them about Ruiz Domingo, that's what everyone called him, I don't know why. A nasty man, really, a brute. When the girl was expecting the baby, he almost threw her down the stairs. D'you know, I thought he was going to kill her . . ."

The woman fell silent for a moment and her voice softened again: "Tell me, is it a big sum she stands to inherit?"

"I can't . . . not a great deal, to be honest."

"You can't tell me, is that it? You're not allowed to?"

"That's right, yes. And the child, did she have it?"

"I dunno."

Her expression went blank, she stepped back out of the light from the doorway and the shadows carved deep lines on her face.

"Are you coming, Baby?" her husband called from behind her.

She put her hand on the door handle and took another step back. At the last moment, she turned toward me, her hands clenching the fabric of her apron, and I met her eyes as they pried into mine, trying to read my thoughts. She spoke differently now, with gentleness in her voice: "I'm glad she's inheriting it, and all that money's going to her, not him. After everything she's been through. It's a good thing."

She stared at me for a long time, without a word, then seemed to reach a decision: "If you find her, tell her . . ."

She shuddered and shook her head. "No, forget that, don't tell her anything, she won't want to come back here. People weren't . . . kind, no, they weren't kind at all. Just tell her to take care from me. My name's Maria Simões . . . No, say it's Pita, that's not my name, but she used to call me Pita. She gave everyone nicknames, that girl, even herself in fact."

"I know . . ." I murmured.

The door was already closed.

THE TASCA WAS on the corner of rua das Tangentes and rua Antunes. It was a seedy drinking hole, forbiddingly dark once you stepped through the sun-drenched doorway. Every couple of minutes, when the Eléctrico W passed, the screech of metal drowned all conversation. The barman was in his sixties with bug-eyes like Peter Lorre. He remembered Ruiz well.

"Did you say Domingo? It's been a long time, hasn't it, oh yes. That's what they called him in the neighborhood, because Sunday was the only day of the week he was just about sober. He used to go to the cemetery, where his wife was buried, so he didn't drink for the whole day."

He thought about this and added with a laugh: "Well, he wasn't drinking here at least."

He wiped the top of the bar with a cloth.

"To be honest," he went on, "it was after she died that he started drinking . . . But hey, I'm not here to stop people from drinking, am I?"

I nodded with a grimace. I hadn't put any sugar in my coffee and it was acrid. Its bitterness was my act of contrition.

"What about his daughter, do you remember his daughter?"

"The little girl? Oh yes, very well. When she was just a kid, she used to come to find Ruiz here in the evenings, when he was too drunk. He couldn't stand up, she even had to put him to bed. When her mother died she must have been, what, about nine years old. She was already a hell of a pretty kid. Is she the one you want or Ruiz? Because I dunno where she is . . . She had some problems, if you know what I mean."

He ballooned his arms over his stomach. I looked away. "And Ruiz?"

"Oh, he comes by sometimes. The last time was about two or three months ago, I think. He used to work in highway maintenance, on street lighting. Mind you, I wouldn't be surprised if he's retired now. Or switched to another job. He was good with his hands."

The barman remembered a name, Custódia. Ruiz Custódia. He also told me where to find his wife's cemetery. In the suburbs. Ruiz used to go there every Sunday afternoon, at around four or five o'clock. But he could have changed his habits, of course.

I finished my coffee, knocked back a glass of brandy, and paid, leaving a good tip. As I was leaving the barman called to me: "Say, if Ruiz comes by, because you never know, shall I tell him someone's looking for him or not? What's your name? Do you have a business card?"

"It's the girl I'm looking for."

It wasn't an answer, but the guy didn't persist.

I WALKED TOWARD the hotel, slowly, feeling slightly nauseous. As the main post office was on my way, I went in. It was cold because of the air conditioning, heels clacked on the floor tiles and conversations smacked against the walls. I looked for the name Ruiz Custódia in phonebooks for all the major cities, and made a note of the addresses. There were no Arcana Custódias, or Arnicas or Arcanis, not anywhere. So, I started making a note of the Adelina, Adriana, Albertina, Anna, Anita, and Augusta Custódias. Twenty-five names in all, in Lisbon alone.

Someone put a hand on my shoulder. I was startled to hear Antonio's voice and dropped my pen like a little boy caught red-handed.

"What are you doing here?"

Antonio was amused to have caught me. He was chewing a sandwich. I leaned down, picked up my pen, and stuffed my notebook in my pocket. He wasn't inquisitive about what I was hiding, but I couldn't help answering.

"I'm looking for an address, I'm trying to call someone. Like everyone else."

"From here? Do it in the hotel."

"In the hotel . . . yes. Are you here to post your letter? Or rather our letter?"

Now I was smiling too. Antonio shook his head: "No. It turns out I won't need to post it. Irene just called. She's coming to Lisbon. In a couple of days. Monday or Tuesday. She'll call. I told her you were here . . ."

He took a bite of his sandwich, seemed to want to gauge the effect he had made.

"Really? And . . . what did she say?"

He stayed silent, an impish crease at the corners of his mouth, and I realized that my speedy response had betrayed my anxiety. He took another bite of his sandwich.

"She told me not to trust you . . ."

He swallowed a mouthful with gusto and looked around.

"I really like post offices, big post offices. The bustle, the echoing voices. It's like the anteroom to the whole world."

He smiled, pleased with his phrase.

"But you see, not like an airport, or a station. There are no departures here, no stopovers. Just addresses,

languages, alphabets, letters and parcels. Absolutely anybody writing to absolutely anybody else. A huge great
phonebook of the planet . . ."

Antonio was pontificating. He threw the last bit of
bread in the trash.

"Shall we go change?"

"Excuse me?"

"For the concert this evening, with Aurora . . . the
Estufa Fria. You *are* coming with me, aren't you? Don't
leave me alone with the sorceress."

He laughed and showed me his palm. There, still shimmering in the light, was the ghost of a blue bird.

AURORA WAS RIGHT, penguins visiting the Amazon was
an accurate image. With advancing years and an accumu-
lation of good port, many of the guests had even achieved
the embonpoint of emperor penguins. I tried to tell Antonio the joke about never competing with Emperor Peng
(because Emperor Peng wins), but he was too busy looking for Aurora to get it, or even listen to me.

"Hey, Vincent, look, there she is. Look how beautiful
she is . . ."

I didn't recognize Aurora in the young woman he was
already walking toward. Perhaps because of the long
cobalt-blue dress, or her hair, which was now not held

in check by any ribbons so it spilled over her shoulders. Beside her was a very tall, very dark, fairly good-looking boy of about twenty wearing a dated gray suit. He was doing his utmost to generate some of the tragic darkness of a Russian soul in his expression. If this were a game of Happy Families, then he could have been the youngest of the Karamazov brothers. This Alyosha spoke very little and smiled very little but never took his eyes off Aurora. She meanwhile seemed distant, a stranger.

When she saw Antonio her face came to life, blossomed. She put a lock of hair behind her ear and abandoned her suddenly powerless companion. She cut through the crowd to reach us, stood on tiptoe and planted a kiss on Antonio's left cheek. Then, in a move that was both intimate and incredibly brazen, she tilted her head for him to return the kiss, in the crook of her neck. He looked helplessly at that shoulder line offered up to him and, as if drawn in by the smell of it, furtively kissed the base of her neck.

"I was worried you wouldn't come, Antonio."

"Well, you can see I have."

I greeted her with a nod, and she skimmed my cheek with her lips.

"Thank you for coming to see me again."

She looked up at the glass roof, where all the ultraviolet lights had been lit.

"Have you seen? Little blue suns . . . I wasn't lying . . ."

She had lost her childish voice and adopted a woman's, but not quite a lady's: "Would you like some champagne? Follow me."

She took Antonio's hand with energy and determination and guided us to the buffet, walking quickly through the dense crowd. Antonio was Aurora's prisoner, leaning forward as he ran after his own hand. Beside the trays of canapés, she finally released him and chose a small pink éclair with sparrowlike voracity, nibbled one creamy end, then put it back down on the tablecloth with a smirk of distaste.

"It's gelatinous and too sweet. Too bad, I really like the color, like a chubby child's finger. Yummy. The concert's going to start soon, I saved you two places, near me."

"Who organizes all this, the concert, the reception?" Antonio asked.

"Well . . . the Philarmonica, isn't it? Why does it matter?"

"Why are you invited? You said your father worked in the hothouse?"

"Have you quite finished with the questions? I've already said, this is my home. Shall we go?"

She took Antonio's hand again and led us to the concert hall. The seats were theater red, the décor rococo. Aurora sat us in our places, 31 and 33, in the middle of the third row of the stalls.

"The best seats, these are. You don't know how lucky you are to know me."

She slipped a program into my pocket with a conspiratorial expression and narrowed her eyes mischievously. She knelt before us, crucifying the fabric of her dress with all the aplomb of a little countess in a silk gown playing in a dusty alleyway.

"Are you comfortable here? I won't be far away, and I'll be watching you the whole time."

She snatched Antonio's hand and opened it like a rose.

"But . . . where's the bird? Did you frighten it? Did it fly away?"

And before Antonio could reply, she was kissing him on the lips and running off toward the wings. After a moment of stupefaction, he looked rather bemused and turned toward me. In the lamplight, his black eyes had gone the harsh green of a hornbeam leaf.

"That girl is . . ."

"Yes, isn't she."

I was smiling, amused by the helplessness on Antonio's face. I was amazed to feel no jealousy at all. Aurora was very pretty, beautiful even, but I wasn't attracted to her. I'm not attracted to women who are too beautiful, because they wear their refusal to seduce like a badge, because a cold hostility seeps out of them, helping them avoid being pestered too often.

And yet Aurora was not a sensual desert. She was well aware of her charms, but tried to please with daring and gentleness. She was sincere and naive, like a girl who doesn't know she has a woman's face and who hasn't yet learned to see herself in men's expressions. To crown it all she had a natural candor that forgave everything else. I would never have dared envy Antonio the tenderness she showed him, because she held the secret to ultimate propriety, she knew how to be desirable to him alone.

The hall was filling up and I opened the simple program printed on a lightweight card. The ensemble was called Quatuor Papageno, they were going to play some Purcell, some Dubois, and some Moulinié. I pointed out a line in the program to Antonio.

"Look, that's where your Aurora's going."

Antonio snatched it from my hand. Among the musicians was Aurora Oliveira, tenor viola. Antonio read and reread those few words, shook his head, and turned to me: "Have you ever heard of a tenor viola?"

"No. Do you think it's like a viola da gamba?"

"I . . ."

Antonio bit his lower lip as if to repress a laugh.

The bell, darkness, one last creak of the seats. As the hubbub died, the curtain rose. A narrow beam of moonlight came through the glass roof. It caressed the smooth face of a young woman standing onstage. Once again I failed to recognize Aurora. I was disarmed to discover how pure her features were, how perfect the oval of her face. Her cheeks glowed with a touch of pink, her lips with a hint of vermilion. Behind her, in the half light, the silhouettes of three musicians were just visible.

Aurora stepped forward, hesitantly at first, like a child about to give a little speech, but her voice proved surprisingly assured: "Moulinié's Fantasy for Four Violas."

She then went and sat in the middle of the quartet. She braced her instrument against her chin, the musicians tuned their instruments one last time, and the concert began.

Antonio never took his eyes off Aurora. I closed mine, to be alone with the music, or perhaps just alone.

I was six years old when I was taken to a concert for the first time. I can remember the rough feel of the worn crimson velvet of the seats, how uncomfortable they were, how my tie squeezed too tightly around my neck. But not the music. It must have been something by Mozart. A child's first concert is always Mozart. I was probably treated to the inevitable: "At your age, little Wolfgang had composed his first symphony," which can convince the most robust that their life is already a waste. I don't remember it.

I have few childhood memories. In the most detailed one, I must be about four. I'm going into a very white villa, I'm wearing shorts that are too big for me, held up by a leather belt that isn't mine. An old woman with dyed black hair hands me a glass of orangeade, but it manages to be both too sugary and too bitter, I pour it over the floor and scream and cry. The woman slaps me, my mother intervenes, defending me. We leave, in a hurry, running over the noisy gray gravel.

That woman doesn't exist, that scene never took place, my mother told me so a hundred times. Even so, this false memory grows more real every year. I know the color of the sky, I can feel the moisture in the hot air, I can still hear the slap of that dry, lined hand on my cheek. Oddly, there is a word associated with this experience I never had, the word "beaver," which meant nothing to me for a long time. To this day I don't know whether that beaver is masking or perhaps belongs to a buried slice of real memories. One day much later, I learned that it was a rodent with large yellow teeth and a strange flat tail. Later still, I knew it was sometimes used to mean a woman's vulva.

I also remember one afternoon in June. June 15 to be precise, because if was my ninth birthday. My great aunt had died a few days earlier. Aunt Odile. I was walking along the sunny street, the rue Lecourbe, where I lived with my parents in a small apartment at number 19, and thinking about Aunt Odile who always smelled of violets, a rather stout, red-faced woman I would never see again. An idea struck me with terrifying force, petrifying me there on the sidewalk with my satchel in my hand: Aunt Odile belonged in the past. I was only nine and yet I had a past, and I existed now because I was aware of it. I went home, devastated by the discovery. I stayed awake all night on June 15, my eyes bulging in the dark. I tried to remember the scene, to rewind back to my summer vacation by the sea, to my last birthday present, but my mind was so abuzz that, in my terror and confusion, nothing came back completely. So in the morning I made a decision never to forget anything again, ever, in order to stay alive.

That is how I was born a second time when I was nine. Before that date of June 15 nothing feels real to me at all. In my own puerile way, I had lived each perishable moment in the present, or rather on the slope of the present that is already sliding toward the future.

I opened my eyes. A smile hovered on Antonio's lips as he watched Aurora play. I realized how much I could loathe this man whose memory was anchored so far out and so deeply, who had been given the gift of existing so early on. If women were drawn to him, then it was because of this past that carried him, making him both lighter and more weighty, a force that told them there was an invisible secret in him, a mysterious "before" that would never be accessible to them.

AURORA JOINED US on the terrace shortly after the concert ended. It was a hot, humid, almost suffocating night, and in the darkness the jungle inside the hothouse seemed to go on forever. Hundreds of sparrows perching up in the palm trees cheeped busily, barely disturbed by the electric lighting.

Aurora had showered, the ends of her damp hair clung to her temples, her forehead was still moist from the steam. A feral child in evening dress. Antonio handed her a handkerchief and she ran it over her face.

"Did you see?" she laughed happily. "Three encores . . ."

She was about to return the handkerchief, but two pale red initials embroidered on it stopped her short. She turned it over in her hand, intrigued. An I and an S.

"I.S.? Like International Socialist? Intelligence Service? Are you an English spy, Antonio? Or is it . . . Irresponsible Savage?"

Antonio took the square of cloth from Aurora's hand without a word.

I.S. Irene Simon. It was Irene's. It was even that same handkerchief, I'm sure of it, that she had waved with a pretense of emotion from the window of a Paris–Rome train one autumn morning. The train was still stationary, she had lowered the window and waggled the piece of white cotton mockingly to point out how ridiculous I was to stay there on the platform. Then she sat down, opposite a young student who was already showing an interest in her, and she pretended to be immersed in some women's magazine.

Her face had disappeared behind a stranger's profile. All that was left in view for me was a fold in the fabric of her jacket, the tips of her gloves, and the colorful carousel of pages as she leafed lazily through them. With a labored creak, the doors closed, the train swayed, and I stood there stupidly watching it move away. The scene tore open like an old bedsheet, I was left empty of all feeling except for my longing for this woman, who was suddenly as unreachable as the distant glitter of those train cars following their tracks on the horizon.

When I remember that handkerchief dancing in the air and that actor's smile you gave to everyone, I realize how much the gesture was calculated to make fun of me and my hangdog eyes. The young man watching you who must eventually have struck up a conversation with you, the ticket collector who helped you carry your cases on board, and even the surly boy in the station buffet, they must all have been privately laughing at me, they had all worked out that you clearly didn't love me.

And yet there were nights when you decided to sleep by my side. I think I amused you just enough for you to want to stay. I spent hours in sleepless torment, inhaling the smell of your body, swamped by your sharp perfume, choked by your heat and coldness like a gnat in a spider's cocoon. I listened to you breathing and couldn't get to sleep, frantic with desire for you. You said you hated that bed where I had slept with other women, I should have burned the sheets, moved house, and you complained when I looked at other women even though you refused to give yourself to me.

Antonio folded the handkerchief and put it in his pocket.

A ripple ran through the crowd and the loudspeakers crackled, started a hum of interference that was quickly stifled. An English blues song came from nowhere, something like Paul Armstrong's "I'm the Flirt of Jesus," and a dozen or so teenagers started dancing on the paved terrace.

Aurora slipped between Antonio and me, and took us by the arm.

"Come on, come and dance . . . it's such a warm evening . . ."

But Antonio took a step back, intimidated, and she pirouetted in front of him. She jigged like a little girl, then began a slow sway with her hips. In the blue shadows above her, with his pair of glasses grafted to a branch, Monstro leaned forward to watch.

Every move Aurora made opened a slit in her dress, her leg was revealed up to the top of her thigh, and Antonio stared irresistibly at her dark skin exposed for a moment and almost immediately hidden. Aurora danced like the jubilant waters of a spring. She was alive, carnal, sensuality itself.

Disconcerted, Antonio stepped backward, apparently wanting to melt into the crowd.

Aurora was dancing, alone, a few paces from him but not with him. She smiled at everyone and no one, and he felt a rush of bitterness, an icy wind that made him back away. The whole world toppled and Antonio understood. She was offering herself to anyone who watched her and wanted her. She didn't belong to him, and he was just realizing that he could lose her at any moment.

Antonio turned to me. He affected indifference, but his unspoken fear had suddenly aged him.

"Do you want to go back to the hotel, Vincent?"

"Didn't you want to dance?"

He shook his head and I remembered *that* night, in Verona, the night when Irene was drunk.

She too danced, stumbling, abandoned, laughing a drunken laugh, flaunting herself on that dance floor, her dress riding up, revealing her tanned thighs, attracting stares, fanning flames. Two men behind me were laughing and talking loudly, one of them used the word *puttana*, whore. I didn't have the courage to hit him, neither did I find the strength to leave, to tear myself away from that spectacle that was nothing but treachery, betrayal. I was drained of all energy, and I stood there, crushed by powerless anger, and watched Irene dance. Of course I could have gotten up, taken her hand, and dragged her off the dance floor, but she would have pushed me away, driven me off, slinging sarcastic comments at me. That night I should have turned my rage to contempt, my defeat to derision, my blindness to strength. I should have left that woman who didn't want to be mine.

Antonio was now also having his doubts that Aurora

had ever wanted to be his, he was finally realizing there was too little in life to connect them, that she would leave one day, was already moving away now, he would suffer, and was suffering already.

Perhaps a man would come and take Aurora by the waist, twirl her around and pull her to him, making her laugh in his arms. Their bodies would touch, their faces would be so close he would have to look away. It would feel as if the other man were possessing her right there in front of him, as if she were abandoning herself to pleasure. This other man would lead her away, taking her arm, and she would hold his hand. She wouldn't even acknowledge Antonio, poor idiotic Antonio, she would have forgotten him already, and he would feel dirtied and then, over time, just dirty. He would want to be left alone to imagine those endlessly repeated moves of fingers and mouths over bodies.

The blues song had finished and the music continued with a slower jazz rhythm, perhaps a Negro spiritual. Possibly Neil Oven's "God Is Sitting on My Knee"? Now that's something Harry would have known.

Aurora was sweating, her skin shimmering like mica, she was radiant with life, a man came up to her and asked her to dance but she shook her head, rejected him with a little bow. She came back toward Antonio and smiled at him, and Antonio's nightmare evaporated. Not entirely, though. Never entirely again.

ANTONIO DIDN'T LEAVE Aurora's side for the rest
of the evening. She had coupled herself to his arm, and
dragged him behind her from one group to another. She
introduced him every time, saying, "Antonio, my friend,"
or occasionally to some people, "my husband."

When people looked astonished she asked indignantly,
"What? Didn't you know? Well, it *is* very recent. Really
very recent."

Antonio tilted his head politely in silence, discomfited, intoxicated. One time Aurora said "my fiancé," and
I smiled.

It was not a well-meaning smile. Talk of fiancés and
engagement reminded me of Stéphanie Poterin du Motel,
Pescheux d'Herbinville's fiancée whose favor Galois had
obtained. If Pescheux and Stéphanie had been married,
perhaps her deceit would have been less hurtful. Cuckold-
ing a fiancé is proof of impatience.

My brother was engaged once. His young intended was
called Virginie, she was twenty to his twenty-two, and
this ritual annunciation of a forthcoming marriage was
almost obscene, in fact between a Paul and a Virginie—
like the book—it was pretty close to ridiculous. But I said
nothing and, at Paul's insistence, even wrote a speech for
the engagement, it was the fashion then.

I reminded them that this promise did not, either in canonical law or contemporary French law, entail any legal obligation to marry. That the engaged couple could indulge in *copula carnalis*, carnal union, but should not forget that if consummated, it was then a case of *matrimonium praesumptum*, a presumption of marriage, and hence de facto marriage.

While I outlined the rules for an engagement, I reminded them that this very expression, rules of engagement, was more usually associated with warfare.

Referring also to Søren Kierkegaard, whose first name I love with that crossed-out ø, Kierkegaard who was engaged to Regina Olsen when he was twenty-six and she barely fifteen, and whose engagement ring he returned three years later. She threatened to commit suicide but eventually found consolation in one Fritz Schlegel. I concluded by saying that this was one of the rare textbook examples where an engagement had ended well, but alas, we did have to face the fact that in most cases the two parties ended up married.

The speech was an unequivocal success. Virginie burst into tears, probably the tension. Paul led me to understand that it had not been what he had meant by amusing. Our father, on the other hand, laughed.

Speech or not, Virginie broke up with Paul a year later as the wedding drew near, apologizing and saying she wasn't "capable of such a formal commitment," was "terrified," and would rather "get things in perspective." She had actually been getting things in perspective for several weeks with one Maxime, a pharmaceuticals student like herself. Paul had never been engaged since, and Virginie, who now ran a drugstore in Asnières, had also got Maxime in perspective and married an Aurélien, whom she was probably also cheating on with some other Roman emperor's name.

The hothouse was gradually emptying. I had sat myself on a bench near the water lilies, to make notes. Aurora walked toward me, smiling. Behind her the tiny lights on the vaulted roof shone like newly polished upholstery tacks.

"Are you still translating that Jaime Montestrela? I asked my father and he said the name rang a bell. He took exile in Brazil when Salazar was in power, is that right? Did he write poetry too?"

"Yes."

"My father couldn't find his old copy of *Prisão*. Apparently it's not bad. Hard to translate."

I had no way of knowing. But the obituary in *O Século* ended with these two lines from *Prisão*, which was cited as his founding work:

Num raio de sol, a poeira faz palhaçadas
Mas que idiota pintou o azul entre as minhas barras?

In a ray of sunshine, dust plays the fool
But what idiot painted blue between my bars?

I had been more interested in Montestrela's life than his writing, as if his existence were an interrogation of my own. If a dictatorship took over, would I go into exile like him, like Zweig, rather than bowing my head completely in the face of barbarity? There was a certain honesty in not being ashamed of one's own lack of courage, in knowing oneself well enough to opt for fleeing anticipated submission, which would be as abject as the violence of the tyrant it empowers.

Aurora headed straight off again toward Antonio while the last guests were leaving. Antonio whispered something to her and turned to me with the shifty, embarrassed eyes of a liar: "I'm going to stay a bit longer. I'll be back later."

I went home to the hotel, walking quickly, almost running. It was only when I reached Avenida da Liberdade that I slowed down. I took the photograph of Duck from my pocket and looked at her for a long time in the glow of neon lights. I tried to find a name for the feeling budding inside me, tenderness perhaps, the sort you would feel for a sister far away.

At that very moment Antonio was betraying Duck, and I resented him for it. He was probably betraying Irene first, but I was delighted by that particular felony. His distraction gave me strength. Soon, when Irene was there, he would be indebted to me for my silence.

I translated a few more *Contos aquosos*. I knew that, botched by my anger, they would need reworking later.

In the morning when the waiter brought up breakfast for two—we had adopted the habit of taking it in the large lounge—Antonio was not there. I waited until midday, in vain, and, as it was Sunday, I thought of Ruiz Custódia and the cemetery in the suburbs. So I decided the time had come to try my luck.

DAY FOUR

◾

$\mathscr{P}$INHEIRO

cool breeze was blowing and I shivered in the shade of a cypress tree. Graves seen in sunshine are never entirely melancholy. There's always a hint of life to distract the eye, a blade of grass glimmering, a carefree chaffinch pecking at the ground, a black beetle with heavy mandibles crawling over the gravel. And when graves have no story to tell, we don't linger over them.

A large weathered stone. Família Custódia. Names, dates, and at the very bottom, Maria Custódia, 1934– 1964. The gilding had long since disappeared, the northern corner of its almond green surface was decorated with a brooch of lichen. There was a bouquet of withered mauve flowers, and a slightly muddy, chipped, discolored porcelain plaque. It said TO MOMMY.

Thirty years old. How old would Duck have been? What sort of lies did they tell her that day? That her mother had gone to heaven?

When my mother died I was in London. For an interview, with the chairman of a chemicals company. Mom had gone to the hospital a few days earlier, she was frightened. The doctor took me to one side, shook my hand: "I'm very concerned. Don't go too far from Paris." But I never guessed it would happen so quickly.

I found out she had died when I returned to my hotel very late in the evening. The message left in my mailbox said: "Urgent: contacter le manager. Votre frère a phoné. Concerner votre mère." Their use of French, even this approximate version, was thoughtful. I reread those words several times and went to sit near reception in an armchair that was a little too low for me. I wished I could feel something, feel the tears rising, but nothing came. I closed my eyes, tried to remember her face. I couldn't.

Under my eyelids, red and crimson hydras, almost translucent creatures, reached out their supple tentacles. I discovered the existence of these luminous shapes in my teens, and they had become familiar. They weren't the blotches of color that stay engraved on objects, phosphenes, as I discovered, much later, they were called. They were well and truly microorganisms with lives of their own, capricious undulating specks of life.

Every evening before I went to sleep, I liked to follow their aimless trajectories across what seemed to me to be a microscopic universe, a living primordial soup, a sort of original ocean. When I moved my eyes, the hydras followed the move for a moment, then stopped as if arrested in cloying jelly, before setting off again on their slow drifting. I concluded from this quirk that they were not the product of my imagination, and invented a serious illness for myself, an unknown infection involving giant bacteria. In the end I got used to them. I later learned they were caused by excess fluid in the vitreous humor, common in the shortsighted.

The night I lost my mother, the hydras were everywhere, more mobile than ever in the shifting liquid shadows. They made it impossible for me to reconstitute her features or even find a memory of her, they were protecting me from pain.

I remember the affectedly baleful expression on the hotel manager's face when he came over to me, walking quickly, bending forward slightly.

"Monsieur Balmer?" he asked, speaking French with almost no accent. "Terrible news, monsieur. Your mother . . . Your brother called this afternoon. She has passed away. Please accept my condolences and those of the hotel staff."

I returned to Paris on the first flight the following morning and took a taxi from the airport straight to the hospital.

The driver wanted to chat—about the filthy weather, the staggered rail strike, the traffic—but I said, "I'm sorry, my mother died yesterday, I don't feel like talking."

My words were like a thunderbolt and he stopped talking immediately. There was something comical about this metamorphosis, and it produced the beginnings of a smile on my face. The driver caught sight of it in the rearview mirror, and I immediately resumed my orphan's mask.

When I went into the room where my mother had been laid to rest, I didn't recognize her. Her body looked tiny, with almost no depth to it, drowning in white sheets, like a pale skinny dwarf, a stranger's corpse. Her mouth was open, gaping, as if she were asleep, knocked out by the smell of ether. Her dentures had been taken out, and, discomfited, I looked away from the obscene sight of this toothless old woman with her dry, twisted lips.

My brother Paul was there, along with my father, and they turned to look at me. Paul stood up, put his arms around me, and hugged me with calculated intensity, he was family but not affectionate. I wanted to hug my father but he was still sitting, had made no move toward me.

"I was in London," I managed to say. "For work . . . I'm sorry."

I had spent my whole childhood saying "I'm sorry." Every time, my father would sigh and say, "Well, don't let it happen again." I wished he had scolded me that morning. He could have said, "You'll never change," or even, as he used to, simply sighed, "You may be sorry, Vincent, but don't let it happen again."

Yes, that's what he could have said. But he stayed sitting and stared right at me. His eyes were red, but I knew he hadn't cried all night, that he had just watched over her, unblinking.

He tilted his chin toward the bed. "It's not me you need to apologize to."

His voice was cold, his expression detached, hard, the sort I imagine people use on traitors and cowards, and I knew then and there that he didn't forgive me, would never forgive me.

I heard a crunch of gravel.

An old man greeted me with a polite nod of his head. His Sunday best was outdated, but his tie neatly knotted, his white shirt ironed. He must once have been a strapping fellow, a force of nature, but he looked tired now. In fact, he wasn't all that old. But he was unshaven or had shaved half-heartedly, and the wind was mussing his gray hair.

I stepped back, embarrassed, as if caught committing a crime as I meditated beside that strangers' grave. I moved away to one side and pretended to pay my respects to another grave, the resting place of one Maule Gorma, funny, he was born the same year as me, 1944, and died in 1979. What do you die of at thirty-five? Then I walked toward the gates, slowly. There, sheltering behind a mausoleum, I waited for him.

Ruiz Custódia, if that's who he was, didn't seem to have noticed anything, or even to be surprised. He took the dead flowers from the grave, dusted it off a bit, and laid a branch of mimosa on it in silence. He scrunched up the paper it had been wrapped in and thrust this into his jacket pocket.

I watched the man. He stood there motionless. His lips were moving, but his hands weren't joined, and I thought he can't have been praying, but talking, to his wife, really talking.

Yes, it must have been Ruiz Custódia. To make sure, I hid and called out his name. He turned around, looked for whoever had called him. But that didn't prove anything: that woman over there also turned to look at me.

He stayed by his wife's grave a long time, still talking under his breath. It wasn't all that absurd, after all, at least no more so than going to a cemetery at all, no more ridiculous than laying flowers to honor a few bones.

In the early years, my father also used to go to the cemetery on a Sunday, almost once a month. He would stare at the headstone, reading our mother's name over and over, even repeating it to himself, as if afraid of forgetting it, or of forgetting his pain: Anne Balmer.

The cemetery was miles from anywhere, lost in the northern suburbs of Paris, and I used to take him in my old Saab, when my brother asked me to do it on the pretext that he didn't have time. I would go all the way to the graveside with my father, my eyes lowered, remorseful for my absence on my mother's last day, but also in disgust for this old man mumbling a dead woman's name.

We went there twenty or thirty times and then one morning, because my father's muttering was louder than usual and people were watching us in embarrassment, I whispered, "There's no point coming here, Dad. It just hurts you."

He turned to me, almost spitting in my face: "But that's exactly why I come here, to be hurt. What did you think, that it was for her? She doesn't give a damn now, Annette doesn't, she doesn't give a damn, and you, you think I've gone crazy, don't you, that's it, my own son thinks I'm crazy!"

He took me by the lapels of my jacket and started shaking me, harder and harder, as if he wanted to fight. Then he let go abruptly, I could tell his legs couldn't hold him and he collapsed on the path without even trying to clutch hold of me. There he was on the ground, crying, making little whimpering sounds like a mouse. I didn't recognize him and felt ashamed and frightened, witnessing this old man's madness. Shame, fear. I remember those two feelings, that had been reduced to one. I wanted to help him stand up, brush him down like a child, his pants had slick yellowish mud on them, but he pushed me away.

"Leave me alone. Leave me alone, I tell you."

He stood up, wiped his eyes, brushed off his pants and jacket, and started limping quickly toward the gate.

I followed just behind him. He opened the gate, walked past the Saab, and crossed the street, almost tripping. I was still behind him, watching the street, afraid he might throw himself under the next car.

We walked on until we came to a bistro, a sort of small-town cafe and store, and my father went in. There was a bar, a newspaper stand, and four or five tables, all deserted. At the back, in another room overlooking a grim court-yard, was a large French billiards table with green baize. My father went up to the bar, ordered a draft lager from a man in a gray overall, and went to sit in a corner of the games room. I asked for a coffee.

"Are you together?" the man asked.

I said that he was my father . . . but the man shook his head as if that wasn't an answer.

On the baize, the three balls were set out in their pre-scribed positions, and my father took a cue down from the wall. He drained his beer without pausing for breath and started to play, alone. I drank my coffee in silence, leaning against the wall, watching the balls gliding, my mind blank.

The black ball hit the cushion and missed the white. My father handed me the cue, took down another, and went to the bar to ask for two more beers. One for me. We played, without exchanging a word. My father kept score and ordered the beers; occasionally he sighed, especially when his shot was particularly inept. We must have played for an hour, or a little less. My ears were buzzing, from all those beers on an empty stomach. Toward midday, the cafe started to fill up with regulars, people who worked locally.

My father put down his cue.

"Come, let's eat."

The dish of the day was a too salty portion of salt pork with lentils. He gulped it down in no time, wiped the sauce from his plate with bread, and, when I was only halfway through my meal, put some money on the table.

"Hurry up and finish, Vincent. This place is dismal."

We went back to the Saab. My father reached out his hand. I didn't understand what he meant, I thought he wanted to leave, that this was a wave goodbye. My heart constricted, for a moment I thought in terror: I'll never see him again.

But he was waggling his hand as if wanting something.

"The keys. The keys to your car. Give them here. I'm driving."

He stayed at the wheel all the way to his house, driving too fast and not saying a word. On the corner of the street he cut the engine and climbed out, not in any rush. I was about to start the car up again when he crouched by the door, looked at me for a moment, and just said, "It's fine like this. Don't worry about me. See you soon."

He smelled of beer. I watched him walk away and open his door. At the last moment he turned around, waved, and, I think, winked.

A few weeks later Paul asked him whether he wanted anyone to put flowers on the grave, and was even going to add "for All Saints' Day," but my father waved his hand back and forth vigorously. Over the next five years we never went back to the cemetery with him. Except to bury him, two months ago now, beside our mother.

In the distance, Custódia had put his hat back on his head and walked away.

He trudged heavily. As he passed the bin for flowers, he threw in the crumpled paper, then put his hands in his pockets and hunched over as if he were cold. When he left the cemetery he climbed into an old truck with chipping paintwork. It was still possible to make out the words ETS CUSTÓDIA—PRAGAL. 2800.

I thought that would be enough of a lead, and didn't try to talk to him. Sure enough, in the Pragal telephone book, I found "Estabelecimento Ruiz Custódia. Cabinetmaker."

THAT EVENING I found Antonio leaning on the bar at the hotel, drinking a whiskey. He was talking to the barman, passing the time of day. My eye came to rest on the back of his neck, and I looked at it for a long time.

So, Irene, this was all he turned out to be, this lover of yours. This short little guy, stooped even, drinking with no sense of style, his hair thinning on the back of his head, this guy who didn't even know how to wear a jacket.

As if sensing me behind him, Antonio turned around. He smiled and I returned the smile. He seemed to be waiting for a question, a sign of complicity, but I just sat next to him. I ordered a whiskey too, and then gauged his reaction as I said, "I went for a walk. All the way to the cemetery on the other side of the bridge."

"Took notes as usual?"

He swallowed some of his drink and I thought I detected a hint of mockery in his voice, as if I attached more importance to my notes than they deserved.

"As usual, yes . . . ," I smiled.

Nothing ever drives me to write, I'm not heckled by tides of words. There is so much vanity in it that I write only to feel worthy of my own respect.

And the characters always prevail in the end, the way dreams prevail over life, fantasy over love. Even your face, Irene, is disappearing behind the face of the woman who bears your name here. From one page to the next, I'm drying you out, withering you, and sooner or later you'll be swallowed up by the Irene in this novel, who's so much more alive than you.

"You should go and take some photos there, Antonio."

"In the cemetery? Okay, in a couple of days. Because Irene's coming tomorrow. You're not forgetting, are you? And the Pinheiro trial starts too."

I nodded.

I wonder whether the time has now come to talk about Pinheiro. It may be a digression here, but this story's so odd, anyway. Two years ago, over a period of four months, Lisbon saw a wave of unexplained murders. Thirteen victims of all ages and from every walk of life. A retired old woman, an unemployed laborer, a family practitioner, a fishmonger, a bank employee, a schoolboy . . . There was a link between the murders but the police chose to hide it from the press so no one knew a serial killer was operating in the city: the killer used the same weapon every time, a .30 caliber pistol. And he fired two or three shots every time, not with relentless ferocity, just to be sure the life had been taken.

The investigation was so short of clues that it would have dragged on for a long time were it not for a tailor working late one night who, shortly after hearing two shots ringing around the courtyard of his building, saw a stranger come out of the porch. The tailor rushed outside. The man was walking slowly, not turning around. He wasn't running away. Even so, spurred only by intuition, the tailor caught up with him and held him by the sleeve. Ricardo Pinheiro froze on the sidewalk. He didn't seem surprised. He had "faraway eyes," according to the witness's statement.

He was an insignificant man. He was wearing a gray Prince of Wales checked suit, fraying along the sleeve and the collar, and a gray flannel hat with a black ribbon. Something heavy distended one of his pockets, and the tailor was frightened. He started yelling for help, still keeping a hold of Pinheiro. Pinheiro tried listlessly to free himself, less to escape than as a reflex.

The 7.65mm Parabellum Luger was in his pocket, its barrel still burning hot, and four bullets were left in the cylinder, one of them ready to be fired. He didn't try to use it against the tailor. Meanwhile the grocer's wife on the third floor lay in a pool of blood, the bullet had shattered her skull.

When the police arrived, Pinheiro was lying unconscious on the sidewalk. The crowd must have punched and kicked him until he collapsed, although the tailor said that he fell with the first blow.

He was taken to the hospital, where the doctors made a bizarre discovery: under his clothes, next to his skin, Ricardo Pinheiro was wearing a fine coat of bronze chain mail.

For a week Pinheiro remained in a state of unconsciousness close to coma. Then, as soon as he was questioned by the police, he admitted to all the murders, without providing any explanation. He even admitted to those committed while he had been visiting his sister near Porto. It was the police who found witnesses to exonerate him.

He didn't betray his accomplices. He didn't explain the bronze chain mail or ask to wear it in prison, contradicting every diagnosis made by psychiatrists.

The press was expecting a great deal from the trial, perhaps too much. I thought Pinheiro would say nothing, would let a succession of experts take the stand, attending his own trial without a word, more of a Bartleby than a Jack the Ripper. Keeping a record of his silence suited me very well.

DAY FIVE

■

CUSTÓDIA

he following morning we woke early and worked for nearly two hours on the material gathered in the port: described the rusting metal and oily water, captured the sounds of the docks with percussive verbs and supposedly grating adjectives. Then Antonio looked at his watch and stretched.

"Okay, I need to get to the airport. Her plane lands at 11:50. Are you coming with me? Irene'll be pleased to see you. I'm sure she will."

My head swam and I opted to invent a lunch date.

"Lena's reserved a table at a restaurant. In the Alfama district. If I go with you I won't be back in time."

"Call her, arrange to meet later . . ."

"I already tried to earlier. She'd left the house for the day. No, really, it won't work."

"We could meet up later. For coffee maybe?"

From his insistent expression, I gathered he didn't want to be left alone with Irene, he was weakened by his disloyalty the day before, he was vulnerable. I decided to adopt another tactic.

"Sure. Why not?"

"What's the name of the restaurant?"

"I . . . I don't know its name. Well, I only know how to get there." Antonio smiled sardonically. My ridiculous answers made me a little more suspect. I gave in: "Okay. Come and join us. I'll leave a message for you at the hotel with the address."

Antonio nodded and put on his scruffy jacket.

"Okay, I'm off."

At the last moment he turned in the doorway: "Don't forget. About the restaurant."

I WENT UP to the old neighborhood in the heights, near the Largo Santa Luzia, and chose a table on a terrace just before midday.

I called the hotel to leave the restaurant's name, and told my waiter emphatically that I needed to eat quickly. The plane must have landed, and I was afraid they would appear around the corner of the street at any moment.

To create the illusion of a fellow diner, I put a chair opposite me, spilled some drops of wine and sauce on the tablecloth, scattered a few breadcrumbs, and even marked the white paper place mat with the circular imprints of a second plate and a glass. A Lena could very easily have just left the table.

The successive courses came too quickly, and when the waiter cleared the table, it was barely half past twelve. I ordered two coffees.

"At the same time," I specified.

"At the same time?" the waiter repeated. "Your coffees?"

"Yes, please."

"It's no trouble coming back, sir. Or the second one will go cold."

"No, no, bring them both, it's fine."

He walked away but I saw him raise his eyes to the heavens. When he came back I paid the bill so that it wasn't left lying on the table. I drank the first coffee very quickly, almost burning my mouth.

He wanted to remove the empty cup, but I insisted he not touch it.

"No, no, leave it. I have some friends coming soon."

He looked at me, bemused, and headed back to the kitchen. On the way he stopped to have a few words with the woman at the till. He prodded his temple with his finger, and I realized my eccentricities were being discussed.

Twenty to one. I finished the second coffee and ordered a third.

"Yes, sir. Should I leave everything on the table? All the coffee cups?"

"Please."

"Yes, sir. No problem. No problem at all."

I decided to look away to avoid seeing whether he stopped at the till again. I took out my newspaper and started looking through it, without managing to read it properly.

On the third page, though, a headline filled the entire width of the paper: the Pinheiro trial was about to begin. Two weeks earlier my landlady had mentioned him because he had lived only two streets away.

"You know that Pinheiro worked at the customs office at the docks," she had said. "But he used to have lunch in my son-in-law's restaurant every day, and he never talked to anyone. No one. He used to read the whole time. How awful!"

She had said "How awful!" again with a shudder.

I folded the newspaper, wondering what on earth I could write about Pinheiro. I was bound to find something. Murderous madness in ordinary people is always a good subject.

I was finishing the last of my coffee when Irene appeared around the street corner, side by side with Antonio. She was wearing a floaty dress in bright scarlet that I hadn't seen before, and suede pumps. Before even making out her features, I instantly recognized her provocative saunter, which turned plenty of heads, the way she moved her whole body, that promise of the pleasures it had to offer, a painful reminder of how much she enjoyed seducing people and, even more, refusing her favors. I have never understood exactly what it was about her that made her so desirable and beautiful in my eyes. Is "beautiful" the word?

They came up to me and Irene let go of his arm to take off her sunglasses and feign astonishment. I could tell she was forcing her laughter, wriggling exaggeratedly, aping herself. Her expression felt as false as a magazine cover girl's as she gazes at her own reflection in the lens.

She sat facing me with a smile on her lips, and her first words were "Well, where is she then, this Lena, this Lena I've heard so much about?"

Her tone was mocking, spiteful, but the sound of her voice still had an effect on me.

"Are you hiding her from us? Are you afraid someone'll steal her, or I'll tell her things you don't want her to hear?"

The blood drained from my face and I felt like slapping her, or just saying nothing, getting up and leaving. But I managed to look amused.

"You could say hello before launching your attack, my sweet."

"I'm not your sweet, my love. And I never was."

I was about to reply but, infuriated, Antonio blurted, "Have you finished your little private war, the pair of you?" Then he turned to me and added more soothingly, "Has Lena left already?"

"Just this minute. You must have walked right past her."

"She was that fat blond thing," Irene chuckled, "the one whose jeans were cutting her up the ass." She laughed out loud.

"Irene," Antonio sighed, "what's gotten into you?"

"Nothing, nothing at all. I'll stop. There. Shall we make peace? My sweet . . ."

She held out her hand to me with the forced smile of a poisonous child. I took it and, before she could snatch it back, kissed it, quickly and chastely, in the crook of her palm. It was a gesture of revenge, a form of assault, subjecting her to the touch of my lips; and yet, despite being driven by vengeance, I couldn't help savoring the sweet warmth of that hand, its ripe perfume. Irene was so surprised that she surrendered her hand to me, as if it no longer belonged to her, and I even thought for a moment that I could keep it, that open hand, for an eternity. I let it go, stirred and embarrassed in equal measure, and to disguise my emotion I managed to laugh and say, "There, peace is sealed."

Irene stood in silence, disconcerted. Antonio seemed indifferent, he hadn't noticed anything. He ordered three coffees, and the waiter leaned toward me, looking very worried: "Can I clear away the other cups now, sir?"

WE SPENT THE afternoon wandering aimlessly around Alfama, then headed down toward Rossio. Irene was seeing Lisbon for the first time, and made naive pronouncements about cities and docks and sailors.

From time to time she took Antonio's hand and sometimes, at the Santana viewpoint for example, she even huddled in his arms. But Antonio kept her at a distance. He probably did it for propriety's sake, out of tact toward me. Perhaps also because of Aurora and my presence, which forbade him the cowardly hypocrisy common to men. But also, perhaps, because the way Irene smothered him with her wheedling affection made him uncomfortable, as if he could tell that her primary aim, and I believed this to be the case, was to wound me.

I talked about Pinheiro, and Antonio and I agreed to go to the hospital the following day. I left them at about four-thirty, claiming I was meeting a friend.

"A friend, really?" Irene asked sarcastically.

I didn't reply, making do with a smile.

"I'll leave you, then. Tomorrow at the hotel at about ten?"

"Won't you have supper with us this evening? Aren't you staying at the hotel?"

"No. I can't. Sorry. See you tomorrow."

I shook Antonio's hand and gave Irene a little bow. "Madame . . ."

"No more hand kissing, then?"

I shook my head and, to get away as quickly as possible, stopped a taxi that was heading the other way.

"Where are you going?" asked the driver. I hadn't thought about that. I was about to give the address for my studio when I remembered old Custódia.

"Pragal."

"Whereabouts in Pragal?"

"I don't know. Does Estabelecimento Custódia mean anything to you?"

"No." He looked at me apologetically. "Would the rail station in Pragal be okay?"

"Yes. That would be great."

The taxi set off and passed Antonio and Irene. They were holding hands. She freed hers to give me a little wave, and I thought I detected a note of sincerity in it.

IT WASN'T EASY finding Custódia's premises. It was just a long, narrow, dark shop on the corner of a tiny street. On the dirty shopfront window were the words

EST CU TOD A. MARCE AR A

in discolored letters. The last R was about to abandon its post too, and I smiled as I remembered the notice there used to be above the wooden seats on the Paris Métro, one whose words had filled a few fruitful hours in my teens:

THESE SEATS ARE RESERVED

FOR DISABLED EX-SERVICEMEN

Armed with a good scraper, I had devised a simple literary technique, striving to extract some meaning from that sentence. I found I could turn it into an abstruse culinary recommendation:

HE EATS SE ED

FOR ABLE SERVICE

or a sensational headline:

HE S E E S RED

FOR D SE X VICE

Although my uncontested favorite was the darkly Magrittian:

H ATS ARE SERVED

OR BLED

This game was interrupted by an on-the-spot sixty-franc fine for vandalism, when I had only just embarked on the onomatopoeic poetry of:

THE SEA RE RE RE R E

I didn't know where to go next with this poem, but had calculated that there were about seven hundred different solutions. Fewer than the number of Métro cars, no doubt, and some of them impossibly obscure. But what sort of *Iliad* could anyone get with EST CUSTÓDIA. MARCENARIA?

The cabinetmaker's metal shutter wasn't lowered but the door was locked. I knocked on the glass several times, then, when no one came, decided to take a walk around.

As I passed the local tasca I spotted old Custódia. He was sitting at the end of the room with a glass of red wine, his blue work overalls gray with wood dust. He sat drinking in silence. His paper was open to the financial pages, but he wasn't reading. I went in, stood at the bar and ordered a coffee.

Custódia looked older, more stooped, more tired than at the cemetery, well into his sixties perhaps. His hands were worn and rough but still strong, I pictured Duck's pretty face being struck by them. Four old boys were having a noisy game of cards, using matches to keep score, and staking cigarette butts as bets. Custódia wasn't paying any attention to them. Sitting there bringing his glass to his lips, his eyes were expressionless.

When I asked the waiter if he knew where the cabinet-maker was, he called across the room: "Hey, Ruiz, I've found you a customer."

The cardplayers paused for a moment to stare at me, and the old man turned to look. I took a step toward him, but he made up his mind to stand.

"What do you want? I'm closed at this time of day."

"Closed? At five o'clock?"

Custódia shrugged and headed for the door, in spite of everything. I fell in step behind him. Just before stepping outside, he smacked his hand on the bar to catch the waiter's attention.

"Leave the glass. I'll be back."

"Shall I fill it up?"

"That's right."

THE INSIDE OF Custódia's shop was like its exterior. The color of the walls was unidentifiable beneath a layer of filth, the floor tiles hidden by sawdust and wood shavings. Chisels and moldings were strewn over the workbench, and the air had an intoxicating smell of turpentine and wood glue.

"What's it for, then?"

"I need a piece of furniture . . . a set of shelves. I wanted to get an idea of the price."

"Do you have the measurements?"

"More or less . . ."

Custódia headed for the door.

"Not more or less," he said with a shrug. "I don't work in more-or-less-ness. I need it spot on. I've seen too many of you awkward customers who give me the wrong dimensions and then say I'm dishonest. Come back when you've got the measurements. I'll give you a price then."

He reached for the door and I quickly replied, "Wait, wait, I've got your measurements for you. It's . . . six feet by two feet six inches."

"Is that the height, the six feet?" Custódia asked, staring at me harshly.

A sketchy plan to find Duck gave me the strength to carry on with my ploy.

"Well, that gives you six shelves inside. I'll put four runners in it for you. Is that okay? And how deep do you want it?"

"Um . . . six inches."

"That's pretty deep. Anyway . . . Have you made a decision about the wood?

"I don't know, what about pine?"

"That's not wood," he sneered.

"In . . . in oak, then . . . What do you think?"

"It's for the customer to decide. Oak's hard to cut, but it's no worse than anything else. For the thickness, will three-quarters of an inch do, and half an inch for the shelves?

"Will that be enough?"

"Of course that'll be enough. Otherwise, I'd suggest something thicker."

"Aren't you writing any of this down?"

"No," he said flatly. "Oak, six feet, two feet six inches, six inches. Three-quarters of an inch thick, half an inch for the shelves. There's really no point. Do you want them mortised? With moldings?"

"Whatever's simplest," I said weakly.

"It's no more complicated. Anyway . . . When's it for?"

"As soon as possible. When could you do it for?"

"The day after tomorrow if you want. I'm not going to lie, there's not much work anymore, with all this self-assembly furniture. It's been years since anyone's asked me for shelves. So I've got the time, and the wood in stock. But you'll have to pay half up front. For the oak."

"How much will it be?"

Custódia named a figure that struck me as exorbitant and I wrote out a check without a moment's hesitation. He looked at me oddly.

"You want to pay the whole lot now?" he asked.

"If you like," I replied, not understanding. I took out a second check, wrote out the same figure for the balance, and handed it to Custódia, who tore it up without a smile.

"No, we missunderstood each other. The first check was enough. That pays me for everything," he said, shaking his head. "You're a funny kind of a guy, you really are. Do you have no idea of prices or what?"

"Can you deliver it?"

"Is it in Pragal?"

"No. Lisbon. By the docks."

"Do you have a business card with your number? In case there's a problem?"

"No, I've only just moved," I explained, and wrote my address and telephone number on a scrap of paper. Custódia put it in his pocket without looking at it.

"Right, I'll deliver it the day after tomorrow, in the afternoon, at about three o'clock. Make sure you're there, won't you?"

He turned away and walked off toward the back of the shop. As I left, I'm pretty sure I heard him fart.

BACK IN LISBON, I bought paper, charcoal, and a dark wooden frame, and went back to my studio. By nine o'clock I had enlarged and traced out the portrait of Duck, but back to front to alter the shadows and perspective. I drew her almost naked, hidden by fine tulle, hinting at the outline of her small round breasts. To age her by ten years, I accentuated her features with charcoal. It wasn't an exact likeness, but was all the better for that. At ten o'clock it was hanging on the wall.

I opened *Contos aquosos*. My only discipline was to translate at least two of them a day. That evening I finished three, including one particularly absurd one, sent to someone called Ursula in January 1971:

When January 12 falls on a Sunday, the Picardy village of Abelvilly still to this day celebrates it as the Feast of the Gulerian, when this creature is hunted for the tender meat on its large fleshy ears. The gulerian is a patagrade with a bright orange pelt, similar to a badger in size and a tortoise in mobility and agility, specific to that part of the Caux region and sadly extinct since the first Feast of the Gulerian in the year of grace 1197.

Obviously, each of Montestrela's short stories contained another story which, if not secret, was at least masked from all except the addressee. Perhaps, given that he wrote one a day, he was referring to a trip to Picardy with this Ursula on another January 12, in 1971, for example. What did the gulerian stand for? I didn't have the keys.

At about eleven o'clock the temperature had not yet dropped, and I decided to look in at the hotel. Just for a few minutes, to return the photo to Antonio's wallet and pick up some notes. I think I also still hoped to catch a glimpse of Irene, if only for a moment. They weren't in the bar, I thought they might have gone out for supper, and I hurried up to the room.

I opened the door to my suite. Antonio hadn't closed the double doors between our two lounges, and I saw the sliver of light under his bedroom door. I took one step into the dark room and closed the door discreetly behind me. I saw his coat over a chair, took out his wallet, put the photo back and lay the coat down again. After that, there were just the noises.

The bed creaking, the regular animallike squeak of the springs, a woman's voice I didn't recognize, Irene's voice, moaning, repressing a cry and then failing to contain it, like a cry of pain, and there's that man's bass, unrecognizable, whispering such huge words, words that belong to moments no one should ever hear, words I can't even transcribe here.

I stand there, thunderstruck, rooted to the spot, I'm the foot soldier who's still standing, panting, his guts blown away by a cannonball, who doesn't yet understand that he's dead.

I can hear the heavy breathing, the tension of bodies violently seeking their own pleasure, my chest full of lead and mud. I must leave. I manage to tear myself away from the terror in that room, stumbling in the hallway, crushed, racing down the stairs. I narrowly miss falling ten times, but I'm too desperate to get away to fall completely. I go through the lobby and my flight only stops in the small grayish courtyard in front of the hotel, in front of a bellboy who daren't come over to me. I lean my back against the bare stone and crouch down, my head slumping onto my knees, shivering. The noise and bustle of the city doesn't reach me, there's nothing left inside me except for these incoherent sentences going around in circles.

I blot out all thoughts of that night. But what's the point? At dawn I went back to the hotel, confronted their faces and their eyes, but it wasn't the same bellboy. Anger authorizes resignation and rebirth. I was like a soldier whose fear has been utterly consumed under a deluge of fire and who, because he's no longer capable of anything, becomes capable of everything.

DAY SIX

※

MANUELA

waited a long time in the breakfast room, lei-
surely perusing the *Diário de Notícias* newspaper, then rereading it. They didn't come
down, I went through to the lobby and sat in an armchair,
resting my head against the leather and closing my eyes.

My father was walking up a stone spiral staircase, he was
in pajamas, with mules on his feet, I was following him,
holding a candle, wearing a tuxedo and worried about
getting it dirty in that dark dusty-smelling stairway. The
stairs went on forever, I avoided getting too close to the
walls as if hands might leap out of them and clutch at me.
My father went up without a sound, without even breathing, I was afraid he might turn around to look at me with
his cadaverous stare, blank, accusing, and empty. A hand
gripped my shoulder, I jumped in terror. And woke up.

Antonio shook me, smirked in amusement, went to pour himself a coffee, then thought again and poured a second cup which he brought over to me.

"Sleep well, Vincent? You don't look like you did."

"A neighbor kept snoring. Irene?"

"She's still in bed. Big sleeper. We'll call her later. Come on, we're going to deal with Pinheiro."

I folded up the *Diário* and followed Antonio.

THE PSYCHIATRIC HOSPITAL was a large tall 1950s building with plain architecture, covered in unhealthy ochre-colored stucco that was coming away in large flakes. Ricardo Pinheiro was locked in a padded cell in the security department. A pointless precaution given that, since his arrest, he had tried nothing against himself or his guards.

Dr. Vieira was a short bald man in his sixties, on the chubby side, jovial-looking, with an extinguished cigar wedged permanently in the corner of this mouth. Gray overalls would have turned him into the archetypal hardware dealer, but the white equivalent failed to make him look like a psychiatrist. Scarlet tie, pink-and-turquoise Jacquard sweater: Vieira had plenty of taste. Bad taste but a lot of it, as someone once said. He was talkative too, and I think that, after greeting him, I didn't need to ask a single question. He was proud of his patient, as the director of a zoo would be of a recently acquired rare specimen.

"So, are you here to ask me about our national celebrity? Watch out, don't forget I'm seeing you in my capacity as an expert witness, not in my capacity as practitioner, right? And for the record—and I insist on this 'for the record'—I'm a psychiatrist. I don't want any trouble. I won't breach confidentiality. We're agreed on that."

I nodded.

"Perfect. Pinheiro may not be our first serial killer, but he's the strangest of all. Obviously, because soldiers and doctors don't fit in with statistics, killing is kind of our job, isn't it?"

Vieira pushed his glasses up his nose, loosened his collar, and led us into his office, which was cluttered with files. He sat in his chair, I took the other one, and Antonio got out his camera.

"He's almost a pleasant man, this Pinheiro. Smiley, not disturbing in the least. If he wasn't in pajamas and slippers you'd think he was a visitor or, actually, some cleaner guy, a doctor even. Important, those slippers. They're real proof that . . ."

Vieira twirled his index finger around his temple. He laughed and tucked his cigar in the breast pocket of his overalls, with the glistening chewed end uppermost.

"Here," he said, "a piece of advice. Don't ever put slippers on, they'd never let you out of this place. Okay, I'll show you what there is to see."

Vieira opened a file. Pinheiro looked different in the photographs, he seemed younger, maybe forty, and thinner too. Perhaps due to hospital food, and the year of enforced rest. He never looked at the lens, but always high above it, as if an angel were hovering in the room.

"There's a paranoid aspect to Pinheiro, and this is indicated by, for example, his inability to criticize himself, his sensitivity, even his distrustfulness. But there's no pride or authoritarianism. And at the same time, he presents a schizoid pathology: his solitary, introverted side, which is almost certainly coupled with a vivid imagination—that bronze undergarment was quite something, after all!"

"A coat of mail."

"If you like. Would you like to see it? The police kept the thing itself, but look what I have here."

He riffled through the folder and spread a number of photos on his desk.

The coat of mail had clearly been made using traditional craftsmanship. It would have covered his entire torso from the small of his back to his neckline, and was so heavy it must even have injured him. I obviously pulled an expressive face because Vieira clarified: "Seventeen and a half pounds. And no tools to make a thing like that were found at his house. In fact, did you know that on his wrists and ankles he wore plain bronze hoops, no ornamentation or engraving? Even sewn into the felt rim of his hat, guess what we found? A wide band of very thin bronze."

He shook his head.

"I warned all the staff. Paranoid schizophrenics are unpredictable creatures. You know, a guy like that could eat your eyeballs! We didn't get a thing out of him, he didn't want to talk about anything. The only conversation I managed to have with him was about astronomy."

"Astronomy?" Antonio asked as he put away his camera and films.

"Jupiter's moons, it was his favorite subject. Pinheiro says that on a dark night with a clear sky, fewer than one person in a thousand can see them with the naked eye. Which might as well be no one. Before the astronomical telescope was invented, anyone who *could* didn't dare talk about it."

"Was his eyesight really that good?" Antonio asked in amazement. "In the pictures though, he's wearing little glasses, look."

"No, I think it was actually his favorite metaphor. He told me several times, 'Be right about something one day in front of everyone, you'll be taken for a fool for a day.'"

Antonio closed the zipper on his bag, his noisy way of showing he wanted to get out of the hospital as quickly as possible. Vieira noticed this impatience, closed his file, and politely claimed he needed to leave for his consulting hours. He shook our hands and was already walking away, but turned around and handed me his card.

"If you're alone in Lisbon . . . It's only a small place, we might bump into each other by chance, but should we always leave everything up to chance? Do you have a card?"

I told him what I had told Custódia: "I've only just moved."

IRENE ASKED US not to wait for her, and we had risotto for lunch on a restaurant terrace, in the shade of a large ficus in a square along Dom Pedro Avenue.

When we were having coffee, an Irene in a red dress appeared around the corner of the street, facing me, suddenly looking heavier than I remembered, almost plump. She waggled a copy of *Le Monde* in her hand, ran over to us, and, without a word, nestled on Antonio's lap, taking his hand and putting it on her bare thigh. Then she gave me a fish-eyed stare, drained of any expression. I looked at my watch, miming someone in a hurry, and stood up. Irene rested her head on Antonio's shoulder.

"What? I just get here and you're leaving? Your Lena again . . . This is obsession or I don't know what I'm talking about."

"Exactly, you don't know what you're talking about."

I smiled at my own retort, because I'm so often several beats behind. To leave things on that victorious note, I said goodbye to Antonio and left immediately.

I walked along Dom Pedro Avenue, a small street leading down to the port, and stopped to look at the window display of a curiosity shop, intrigued by a Dogon statue, or it could have been Tellem. It was likely to be fake but had an interesting patina. I went straight in.

The only valuable object I had in Paris was an Inuit mask hanging on the wall in the living room. It was large, made of driftwood with feathers stuck into it. It most probably represents a seal or even a seal-man with its red teeth and dilated nostrils. It would have been a ceremonial mask worn by a shaman to ask the spirits to ensure that the caribou, which headed south in winter, would return the following summer. Its first buyer was the Reverend Samuel Wallis. He drew it in his diary for 1897, which can still be consulted in the library at the University of Victoria (British Columbia). Next to the sketch, Samuel Wallis has written the date—February 17—and that he bought the mask for a dollar from a trapper who was asking five. The mask had been found at about Christmastime, to the north of the Kuskokwim River, in an Inuit cemetery, next to a man's corpse that the foxes had unearthed and half eaten. Wallis wrote that the trapper had put the body back in its grave under a pile of stones and secured the mask to his sled with the beaver pelts, then urged his dogs on through the dusk of unbroken night over the frozen waters of the Kuskokwim, to sell his furs in Mamterillermiut. The name means "the people of the smokehouse," because they smoke fish there. It was just a village with about a hundred inhabitants, at the mouth of the river, a few dozen miles from the Bering Sea: mostly Inuits, but a few white men too, gold diggers, traders, missionaries from the Moravian church, including the Reverend Samuel Wallis. A few years later Mamterillermiut would move to the western bank and be renamed Bethel; in 1905 a branch of the U.S. Post Office would open there.

When I looked at that Inuit mask I often thought of the Reverend Samuel Wallis, of the application with which he drew it in his diary. Outside, it had been dark for five months, blizzards whipped up icy snow, he could hear it beating against the walls and windows of the mission. He had seen plenty of other masks, fish masks, masks depicting beluga whale hunts, fox or bird masks. He must have stopped wondering about these sculpted wooden faces by this stage. It was now the masks that questioned him. They certainly wouldn't have toppled his faith, but he saw too many of them not to be disturbed. The Reverend Samuel Wallis probably couldn't quite explain these unsettling feelings. So many different peoples had shaped pieces of wood. Perhaps the question the Reverend Samuel Wallis asked himself was "Why am I so far from home and yet so close to myself?"

I wandered around the store. A tall fair-haired man was cleaning a fragment of stained glass in a frame. I asked him how much the Dogon statue was. It was far too cheap to be authentic, and therefore far too expensive for a fake. I dawdled a little longer, chatting to the salesman, an American who had recently moved to Lisbon, when, reflected in a mirror, I could see the sidewalk on the other side of the street, and Irene. If it hadn't been for the too red dress, the brief dazzle of it in the sunlight, I wouldn't have noticed her.

I freeze where I am, just to be sure. It's definitely her, hiding behind a truck. Irene's following me.

I leave the store and head toward Rossio, checking reflections in shopwindows for my tracker on my heels. It doesn't occur to me to shake her off. As I pass the Café Brasileira, I decide to sit at a table on the terrace and pretend to be surprised when I see her. But at one of the tables is a young woman with brown hair cropped very short, wearing jeans and a white T-shirt; she looks up and gives me a hint of a smile. She brings her coffee to her mouth, the movement ethereal, fine as an italic letter. I catch a glimpse of a tattoo on the inside of her wrist, a tiny turquoise dolphin, small enough to be hidden by a 100-escudo coin, not unlike the dolphin etched onto my black notebooks. That is when, with no plan or idea in mind, I do something that amazes me.

I go over to her. Her lips are thin but they form an O of surprise when I sit in the wicker chair opposite her.

"Excuse me, please let me sit down, I won't stay long."

She's startled, she tenses imperceptibly, looks at me irritably and shrugs. She reaches for her packet of cigarettes and I can tell she's going to get up and leave.

"Please," I say quickly, "I beg you, don't get up. Don't be frightened."

"I'm not frightened."

She hesitates for a moment, my eyes are beseeching, I've no idea what I look like right now.

"Promise me you'll listen to me just for a minute. Please."

She takes a cigarette and lights it. Her reaction was only hinted at, Irene can't have grasped it. She might think the woman's impatient gesture was because I'm late. The young woman looks at me, hesitant, amazed, no—better—intrigued. She has fine, charmingly irregular features, her nose perhaps not quite straight. I detect a note of amusement in her expression. Anyway, I can't be that disturbing, dressed in the "sensible student" clothes I've never stopped wearing.

"I'll explain. I don't know where to start. I'm Vincent, Vincent Balmer. I'm French."

"That's obvious, you have a French accent."

She shrugs, tilts her head to one side prettily.

Her eyebrows go up and form a tiny crease across her forehead. She pushes her brown hair off her face without a word. Eventually she smiles and shakes her head, pouting impatiently.

"I—I work here," I stammer. "In Lisbon. The woman watching us at the moment is . . . is a girlfriend. An ex-girlfriend. She left me. She thinks—well, actually, I'm making her think—I have a girlfriend here. A partner, if you like. But I don't know anyone in Lisbon, I mean, I don't have a friend . . . a woman. And right now she's following me because I said I was going to meet my girlfriend. I'm sorry, I do realize this is all quite muddled . . ."

She eyes me in silence, rather sternly.

"Yes, you do seem muddled." Her voice has a slightly cracked, hoarse quality, but a singing lilt. "Is she still there, this woman?"

"I don't know. She must be behind me, pretending to look in shopwindows."

She stretches her neck to look over my shoulder.

"No, don't look," I almost shout.

"Listen, there are dozens of women looking in shopwindows. How do you expect me to believe your story? Do you often hit on girls with a fabrication like that?"

My expression is so pitiful that a crease of amusement hovers over her lips.

"Okay, let's go with it. And why did you tell her you had someone?"

"Because she left me. To show her I was over it, I'd forgotten her, because I loved someone else. I don't know, to keep up appearances in front of her. Or maybe to see if she was jealous."

She stares at me intently.

"You are sure she was following you, aren't you?"

"Absolutely, I swear it."

"And what does this woman look like?"

"I don't know. She's short with curly brown hair."

She can't help smiling, there are lots of short women with curly brown hair. I have a flash of inspiration: "She's wearing a dress, a really very red dress, with flouncy bits. And a necklace of orange, blue, and black beads. I gave her that necklace. And . . . I think she's still holding a French newspaper."

She picks up her coffee cup, takes a small sip, then puts the cup back down. Without looking up, she says: "There's someone who exactly matches your description behind you, she's admiring some glass jugs in a window. One point to you."

"You see, I'm not lying."

"Mmm . . ." She stares at me sardonically, a touch of pink on her eyelids heightens the green of her eyes. It's quite ordinary makeup, but she hasn't overdone it.

"Or she's your accomplice," she says. "That's it. You arrange these setups together. You do it for her, she does it for you." I must be looking desperate because she adds: "Okay, okay, I believe you."

She lowers her sunglasses and stops talking. I can't make out her eyes now and guess she's secretly watching Irene.

"She's very young, your girlfriend . . ."

"Twenty-two, twenty-three, I think."

"Like I said."

I blush, this stranger is in a good position to spell out the truth to me.

"So then, I'm meant to be your mistress, am I? Am I meant to have a name?"

"I told her about a Lena . . . Lena Palmer."

"She sounds like a heroine from a TV series."

"It's—it's meant to be your husband's surname. You're . . . you're going through a divorce."

"What about you? What's your name? I know you've already told me, but I was angry and I don't remember it."

"Balmer."

"Balmer . . . And I'm Palmer, is that right?" she asks. "That's completely ridiculous. And what's your first name, you fool. Do you really think I'd call the man of my life by his surname?"

"Vincent."

"Vin-cent Bal-mer . . ." she lets the syllables hang in the air, to let their perfume take hold of her. "And I'm Manuela. Manuela Freire. Your story's totally absurd. Which is why I believe it. It's like Catholic faith . . . *Credo quia absurdum*, right?"

She stops talking, slips her sunglasses onto the top of her head, and looks at me for a long time. It's then that I realize I dared approach her and embark on this because her face looked familiar, you could even say like a friend.

If she were seventeen with slightly longer hair, she could be the twin sister of the very young actress in *Thirty Years Without Seeing the Sea*. That first feature by an unknown filmmaker enjoyed far too little success, but the actress took it to heart. What was her name? Clémence Guatteri? Constance Guettari? It doesn't matter.

The story is easily summarized: a teenage girl, probably running away from home, sets off from an anonymous suburb, hitchhiking her way to meet her boyfriend in northern Germany, in Lübeck, where he works as an apprentice chef in a French restaurant. Filmed in parallel is the story of a Polish hitchhiker in his thirties armed with a tourist visa—secured God knows how—who arrives on the outskirts of Paris, on the last leg of his journey to the Mediterranean which he's dreamed about his whole life. They meet at a gas station. She's been caught stealing biscuits by the manager, who's about to call the police, so the man steps in and pays for them for her. He instantly falls in love with this very young girl and when she tells him she's going to meet up with her boyfriend in Lübeck, he says he's heading home to Gdańsk. Lübeck isn't far out of his way, and he suggests they travel together. During those few days traveling he protects her with great tact, aware of how lost and yet determined she is, how full of confidence but ready to snap like a thread stretched too tight. And yet she is so luminous and expects so much of life that she is the one to show him the world. She talks and he just listens, fascinated, never admitting his profound distress. He feels his love for her is forbidden, scandalous, and he suffers at the thought—or the impression—that he's too old to deserve her. She's drawn to him, but too inexperienced to interpret her confusing feelings. When they arrive in Lübeck and, in front of him, she calls her boyfriend to announce jubilantly that she's there, the Pole realizes the boy wasn't expecting her, doesn't want her anymore. She hangs up and bursts into tears, he comforts her and she's ready to give herself to him, in despair, in a desperate craving for tenderness too, but he loves her too much to want her at that price. He offers her a train ticket back to Paris. She accepts, they exchange an awkward kiss on the station platform, and she steps onto the train, distraught. He doesn't have enough money left to see the Mediterranean, and hitches a ride home. He actually lived in Lublin, much farther south than Gdańsk.

Thirty Years Without Seeing the Sea is a succession of sensitive, allusive tableaux. The filmmaker must have been fresh out of film school: the framing, camera movements, and even the film's rhythm betray its influences, from Tarkovsky to Nicolas Roeg, but in the arts there is no sentiment more stupid than a fear of being influenced. The film ends with a very long tracking shot: the girl standing in the train corridor, her cheek resting against the window, her eyes dry and red, watching the rain. Then the camera gradually pans, and the shot is no longer lost in a drowning landscape but begins, as the girl herself does, to see a new landscape appear. The sky is clearing, the sun's going to come out.

I remember sitting alone in the darkened room, seeing how intense and dazzling that girl was, suddenly filled with the conviction that I had never truly lived, and I couldn't help my tears flowing.

Manuela Freire has the same fine features and radiates the same charm. Yes, ten or fifteen years later, that runaway teenager, now grown calmer, serene even, could easily cut her dark hair and look like her sister.

I make an automatic nervous gesture, bringing my fingers up to my mouth. Manuela raps her index finger sharply on the back of my hand.

"You could at least stop biting your nails, it's disgusting. Do you know, your friend's completely fascinated by a hideous cherry-red butter dish? What's her name, by the way?"

"Irene."

"She's not bad. Well, if you like that type. That girl's the sort to fuel a few fires. I'm guessing she showed you a thing or two, didn't she?"

She takes a sip of her coffee, watches me cheerfully.

"Ah, she's moving a bit. O-kay. She's moved a whole yard. Now she's completely focused on a soup tureen. Does this Irene of yours like soup?"

"E—excuse me?"

"Soup. S-o-u-p. Broth, consommé, bouillon?"

"I—I don't know."

"You don't know? Now, that's a bad sign. You have to know everything a woman likes and dislikes, if you want to keep her. How old are you?" she adds, frowning.

I hesitate for a moment. "Thirty . . . thirty-nine."

"Really?"

She knits her brow like an angry schoolteacher and I stammer awkwardly, "Yes, yes, I promise you, it's true, I'll be forty in June, next year."

She laughs properly for the first time. She has pretty little teeth in perfect ivory.

"It's okay, I believe you, I believe you. In fact, I'm even going to pay you a compliment, it'll relax you: you look younger than that. I'm thirty-three."

She reaches for her sunglasses on top of her head and brings them down to the bridge of her nose. Not seeing her eyes makes me uncomfortable, I feel more and more at her mercy.

"And, just out of curiosity, why did you choose me?"

"Well . . ."

"There wasn't much choice, is that it?"

I'm fumbling for words, but she's not waiting for an answer: "Aha, your wannabe Sherlock Holmes has now moved to the other side of the store, and because it's on a street corner, she's watching us through the windows."

She catches the waiter by the sleeve, with all the familiarity of a regular, and orders a coffee.

"Would you like one too? You're paying for the coffees. It's just we've been here awhile. I'm back at work at four o'clock. And I have some shopping to do . . ."

"I'm—I'm so sorry. Do you work nearby?"

"Yes, right there," she says, pointing to a large stone building which looks like a stock exchange.

"At the theater."

I think I understand now: "So, you're an actor?"

She laughs. "Yes, yes, an excellent actor. I play the part of the chief accountant every day. They all believe in me."

She tenses her biceps, Hercules-style.

"Hey, I can't see your girl anymore. She must have given up. Or maybe she's taken up another position without my noticing. So, shall we go and do my shopping, then? After we've had coffee. Tell me about yourself."

THE QUARTER OF an hour it takes to drink a coffee is enough to sum up a life—mine, anyway.

If we don't drown ourselves in details, it gives us a not unhappy childhood in Lyon between a fairly absent father, a manager in a bank branch, and a Portuguese mother who taught primary school; not very turbulent teenage years in Paris; history studies culminating in a master's degree; and a small gift for writing which earns me first some freelance work for newspapers, then a job with a daily, in the arts department and later the society section. As for love, a few relationships that never lasted, meeting Irene, her rejection which made me crazy about her. Lastly, my father's suicide, just two months ago.

I didn't hide anything, embellish or blacken anything either, nor did I try to submerge less glorious episodes in misplaced humor. I also related the one notable event: that lost M16 bullet in Nicaragua. A couple of inches farther to the right and writing my obituary for the paper wouldn't have been an easy job. I found it soothing to share these confidences sincerely. I also mentioned the novel about Pescheux d'Herbinville that I kept going back to, and my translation of Jaime Montestrela's *Contos aquosos*.

"The what? By who?" Manuela asked.

I took out the book; she slipped her sunglasses back onto her head opened the book in the middle, and didn't land on the best of the tales.

In the town of Chiannesi (Umbria, Italy), on Shrove Tuesday, it was customary for every inhabitant to swap minds with another, women played at being men, children being parents. This swap included animals, and mice could be seen toying cruelly with cats. The municipality brought a definitive end to this custom in 1819, when the swap between cows and flies led to a crisis.

She handed the book back, not very convinced.

"Are you really translating it?"

"Bit by bit. I like unfashionable authors, the ones who failed to produce a major famous work by which they'll be remembered."

Manuela smiled. She got it. Yes, I feel a sort of kinship with people who fail. Their wanderings forgive my weaknesses, and I don't hate the fact that posterity is so unfair toward them. The wrong done them absolves me from my own inability to create, from my laziness and fickleness.

"What about your novel, what's it about?"

"About the mathematician Évariste Galois and his murderer."

"Is it a detective story?"

"No, Galois really did exist, he died in a stupid sort of duel between two friends, in May 1832. It's thought his adversary was called Pescheux d'Herbinville, but there's another name out there too. In his last letter, written the night before the duel, Galois wrote something wonderful, more about the Republic than mathematics: 'Remember me, because fate has not given me enough life for my country to know my name.' And it's true, his work was found twenty years later. Even so, I'm not getting anywhere with it."

"Finish it by 2032. Then at least you could make the most of the bicentenary." She pulled a face, screwing up her eyes. "You'll notice I'm giving you my most gorgeous smile. She's still there, your Irene. I can see her again, on the far side of the shop, through the glass. I hope I'm pretty enough to compete with her. I'm not too old for you, am I? I *am* over thirty, you know!"

"You're—you're very . . ."

"I'm teasing you, and you're going to say something silly."

Manuela's blue dolphin was leaping over the sun. It intrigued me. She saw me looking at her wrist and this made her smile.

"Ah, the dolphin?"

"Yes. It's very pretty."

"It's a kid's thing. I had it done when I was sixteen, the day after someone very close to me was buried . . . Slit wrists. I was in a terrible state. I had it put right where the razor would go, so that, if I ever had the same idea, the dolphin would stop me. Dolphins save men. Why not women?"

"I'm so sorry."

"It was a long time ago. I don't think I ever really contemplated suicide. I just had my grief inscribed on my skin. An aesthetic act, in a way, almost shameless. Come on, let's go and do the shopping, and you're paying for the coffees."

She stood up, took my arm, and dragged me off.

"It's not unpleasant having someone at your mercy."

WE WENT INTO one of the large stores on the rua do Carmo, and Manuela led me straight to the lingerie department on the second floor. In the still prudish Portugal of the 1980s, the range was hardly exuberant, but alluring underwear has never been my specialty. It was an era of women's liberation, and these emblems of sexual subjection were not part of the seductive palette favored by women I knew.

Manuela couldn't have cared less. She was enjoying asking my opinion about bras and slips. She liked ochre and cream best, ignoring the blacks and purples that dominated that world. Holding a white silk corset with gray-beige lace edging, she leaned toward my ear.

"I'm going to abandon you, you'll know why in a minute," she said, and was just disappearing into a fitting room when Irene appeared.

"You? here? Are you playing the dirty old man in the femme fatale department?"

"I'm with someone. Anyway, you're here yourself."

"I saw you . . . I was over there, in another department."

She waved vaguely to a place behind her where nothing was going on. A glance toward the fitting rooms betrayed her.

"I didn't know you liked this sort of thing," she grimaced, picking up a red leather bustier. "So, would it turn you on if I wore something like this? With garters too?"

I was saved by Manuela's tousled, smiling face peeping between the curtains.

"Vincent? Come and tell me if it suits me. Miss, this size is really very generous, would you have the next size down, a size four?"

She talked quickly and Irene didn't speak Portuguese, but she did understand the mistake.

"I . . . Tell her I don't work here," replied Irene, not so much annoyed as disconcerted.

"Oh, I'm sorry, Mademoiselle," Manuela said in pretty presentable French. "Well, Vincent, are you coming or not?"

I moved closer. She opened the curtain and pulled me by the collar, almost lovingly.

"You speak French?" I breathed.

"No. I have a smattering." Then she went on more loudly so she would be heard, "So, do you like it on me? Tell me the truth. I don't look too much like a hooker?"

I tried to stare at the wall but the corset molded her too wonderfully for my gaze not to linger on the unsettling shadow between her rounded breasts, her buttocks, her very long, slim legs. I stammered some sort of reply and she whispered, "How did you like the bit about the size four? Brilliant, wasn't it? Okay, you've fed your eyes long enough, you great pervert."

"It's feasted. Feasted your eyes."

"Go on, scram. The show's over."

I stepped backward and returned to where Irene was. She said nothing for a moment, then couldn't hold out any longer.

"Is she your Lena, then?"

I could tell from her voice, it was artificial, had too much of a singsong to it: Irene was jealous. Not a lover's jealousy, which would have been colored with pain, just the disappointment of a woman who loathed no longer being the center of attention. I pretended not to notice.

"Yes, it's her. I realize you're seeing her in . . . the circumstances are . . ."

Manuela popped out of the fitting room. She had put on her jeans over the corset. And managed not to look ridiculous. She came straight over to us and gave us a twirl like a ballerina.

"It's a bit expensive. But everything's too expensive when you don't need it. I'm keeping it on. I'll start a fashion."

Then, finally deigning to look at Irene, she asked, "Do you know each other? Come on, Vincent, aren't you going to introduce your friend? I'm Manuela . . . ," she said, not waiting for my reply.

I must have paled, or perhaps Irene showed some sign of surprise, because, with no hint of embarrassment, Manuela added seamlessly, "But people also call me Lena."

"Irene. But people also call me Irene."

It was said provocatively, but Manuela laughed and held out her hand; Irene, caught out, had to shake it. Manuela then went off to pay, and Irene watched her, as a fox might watch a hen.

"Have you told her about me? About you and me?"

"No." And, with as much detachment as I could muster, I added, "Why would I?"

Manuela came back over to us, smiling happily, and took my arm.

"Let's go back to the Brasileira. Do you know that's where Vincent held my hand for the first time, oh, how long ago was that now?"

"Two months," I said quickly.

"Two months? I can't believe it, it sometimes feels like two hours . . ."

We sat at the same table. Manuela took her role remarkably seriously and had fun terrifying me by talking the whole time. She certainly had a smattering of French. When Irene proved too inquisitive, she dropped her head on my shoulder, unaffected and complicit, and let me do the lying for her. Then she steered my stories toward the truth. Divorced? It came through "just two days ago, phew!" The banker ex-husband was called Palmer, almost the same as my name? "Let's change the subject, I'm Miss Freire again now, and things are a lot better like that." Restoring paintings? She was bored of it now, too many issues with ignorant, tyrannical customers, and then there were museum conservators who were "so temperamental, I mean *so* temperamental. One time, this is the latest time it happened, it was at the Louvre—with a Titian." And her own painting wasn't going very well. Nonfigurative work that doesn't see itself as conceptual is "over-over-over. I should be doing conceptual figurative stuff. But I'm still painting theater sets. Especially white walls. I love white walls." As for the accountancy job at the theater, her new financial situation meant she "couldn't turn it down. Accountancy's how I met my husband. Ah! Didn't we say we weren't going to talk about him anymore?" In fifteen minutes Manuela Freire had succeeded in superseding Lena Palmer.

"How about you, Irene, what brings you to Lisbon?"

But there was a cold gust of wind and Manuela looked at her watch.

"I'm sorry," she said, standing up. "I have to go. The curse of the wage earner. See you soon, Irene, it's been a pleasure. Vincent, will you come with me for a minute?"

I obliged, not sure what to do. But Manuela Freire knew. She positioned herself so that Irene wouldn't be able to see her behind me, then pressed my cheeks between her hands, crushing my face so that it probably looked ridiculous and flabby. Then she came right up close till her nose brushed against mine, and whispered:

"Bet this looks like a real lovers' kiss, don't you? I want a detailed report tomorrow with my free cup of coffee."

She turned on her heel and headed toward the theater. A cool raindrop fell on my hand. I went back to sit next to Irene. The sidewalk in front of us was suddenly covered with little patches of darker gray. They were born as round as coins and, wherever there was a slope, they lengthened into teardrops. All at once there was a flash of lightning, immediately followed by thunder, the stiff breeze made the whole town clink and clatter, and the heavy air took on a cooler color. A clear pattering sound came from the ground, everything darkened suddenly, and the rain started pelting down. It quickly invaded the street, dense and luminous, a shivering translucent jelly reflecting the silver of the sky. It could have been monsoon rain, both violent and gentle, cleansing the earth. But no one in Lisbon displayed the defeated nonchalance of the tropics. Everyone wanted to avoid the deluge, taking refuge under shop awnings and bringing in washing that was hanging on balconies.

Manuela was walking across the square in the shower, not rushing, already soaked, her dark hair clinging to her forehead. She tried to avoid puddles, but water streamed everywhere in wide rippling flows. So she bent down swiftly and, in a spectacularly graceful move, took off her pumps. Then she started to run barefoot toward the theater. I must have smiled inadvertently because Irene shrugged irritably.

The storm didn't last. When Irene wanted to go back to the hotel, I didn't offer to go with her. She left alone, turning around twice, as if wanting to test my indifference. But it wasn't faked, and I was all the more surprised for that.

"GALILEO DISCOVERED THE four largest of Jupiter's many moons thanks to his telescope: Ganymede (which is larger than Mercury), Callisto, Io, and Europa. Anyone who claimed to have seen them by night prior to this was deemed mad."

That was how I started my first article about Pinheiro, and faxed it straight from the hotel. Four pages of it. I had indicated that I would write at least three articles: "Jupiter's Moons," "The Man in Bronze," and "The Silent One," covering every aspect of the investigation and Pinheiro's personality. Then I had promised myself that, if need be, I could come back to the trial.

The editor called straightaway: "What the hell's all this junk about Jupiter's moons? The press hasn't talked about any of this. A correspondent's job isn't to go investigating but to read, conflate, and suggest. Read, conflate, and suggest. And that's it. Still, we'll publish the article the day after tomorrow all the same. The others at a rate of one every three days. It's good. Carry on like that. Say well done to Flores for the pictures."

And he hung up.

It was dark, the air warm, and Irene decided we should eat outside on a terrace and, most importantly, we "had to have lobster" because the way they cooked it here was "adorable." Antonio suggested a restaurant in the pedestrian area near the rua São José, where crustaceans in window tanks frolicked gleefully although the most elementary understanding of caution would have required discretion.

We had placed our order and were drinking *vinho verde* while we waited when I noticed a young woman watching us. She was wearing black jeans and an AC-DC T-shirt, her spiky hair was set with gel like the punks in London's Soho, and her eyes were ringed with heavy eyeliner. Because of the getup it took me several more seconds to realize she was Aurora. Even though I had proof of this from the man by her side, Alyosha Karamazov, the tall, brooding young man who clearly followed her wherever she went, standing there stiffly in his perennial gray three-piece suit. Aurora waved to me, but when Irene kissed Antonio she couldn't contain a pained smile, and she moved away quickly, almost running, trailing her attentive escort in her wake.

A quarter of an hour passed and our lobsters arrived. Another Aurora appeared at the end of the street, wearing a long, black silk dress and blue ballet shoes, her hair smooth and still damp from her shower. Alyosha, let's call him that, was still escorting her, taking large strides while she almost ran. Aurora was holding a violin case in her hand. When she reached us, she noticed a wooden crate abandoned outside the metal shutters of a greengrocer's, and dragged it over to the restaurant terrace. The wood rasping on the road surface attracted the attention of the whole street. Irene was first to turn toward the sound with a grimace, then Antonio. I saw him freeze, petrified.

Aurora turned the crate over. It must once have contained oranges, it had the word "Jaffa" on it. She tested how firm it was with her foot and leaped onto it in one swift movement, standing with her feet along the edge. She waited for an amazed silence to descend, then laid her violin on her shoulder and wedged a cotton cloth on the chin rest.

"Heinrich Wilhelm Ernst's Caprice for Violin on Schubert's 'Erlkönig' . . ."

The chin rest was set very high, and Aurora hardly had to lower her head to secure the instrument, which looked like an alto next to Aurora's tiny form in that black dress. She touched the strings twice with her bow, made a small adjustment to one peg to tune the E, and launched into the music with childlike energy, her bow fluid and active. The first staccato sequence implied this caprice would be an incredibly complex, virtuoso piece. Aurora mastered it perfectly. She didn't look at Antonio, she had closed her eyes, concentrating, with a vertical crease down her forehead. On her temples I spotted an area of powder that the water had not quite cleaned away.

It took a matter of seconds for the violin to eclipse all conversation. A woman being heavy-handed with her fork was treated to an eye-popping stare by her companion, and put down her cutlery. The waiter stopped taking orders and leaned against the window. He stared at Aurora, open-mouthed. The very thrum of the street came to a stop. Antonio couldn't take his eyes off Aurora. Irene silently plowed on with her half lobster.

Balancing on the wooden crate, Aurora drew a pure yet fragile sound from her instrument, like a soprano at the peak of an aria, but there was not a moment's fear that she might fail. She allowed herself no leeway, even frowning and going back over a difficult passage where she alone could possibly have known she had gone wrong. I realized that Aurora could not cheat, that it wouldn't have occurred to her. This deep-seated insistence on truthfulness was her trademark, her nobility, and her strength. It's a cliché, I know, but the only image that came to me was of a princess on an orange box.

I sneaked a glance at Irene. I loathed wanting her so much, hated the violent appetite that urged me to look over at her Medusa eyes, the indolent back of her neck, her bare legs, her ass—no other word seemed more apt. For my desire was now tempered with contempt, a scheme to have her and humiliate her. If Irene had let me touch her that day, I wouldn't so much have made love to her as taken her, avidly and vengefully, with no tenderness or feeling. Perhaps she detected this brutality in me, perhaps the evidence that I wanted her so badly drove her still further from me. I had even imagined every detail of this carnal scene and written the whole sequence in my notebook, so that I could realize it in a dream on paper and get it out of my system, but the words were so crude and violent they only increased my frustration and torment. I haven't copied out any of that ignominious sequence in which I abased myself even more than her.

Aurora stopped playing abruptly, and everyone clapped for a long time. But she did not step off the crate. With her violin in one hand and her bow in the other, she waved and said simply,

"A poem by Fernando Pessoa. 'Autopsychography.'"

O poeta é um fingidor.
Finge tão completamente
Que chega a finger que é dor
Ador que deveras sente.

E os que lêem o que escreve,
Na dor lida sentem bem,
Não as duas que ele teve,
Mas só a que eles não têm.

E assim nas calhas de roda
Gira, a entreter a razão,
Esse comboio de corda
Que se charma coração.

The poet is a faker
Who's so good at his act
He even fakes the pain
Of pain he feels in fact.

And those who read his words
Will feel in what he wrote
Neither of the pains he has
But just the one they don't.

And so around its track
This thing called the heart winds,
A little clockwork train
To entertain our minds."

There was some clapping, Aurora played a short legato
and I thought she would step down and bow, but she carried on: "I recited that poem by Pessoa, it's . . . one of
his most famous poems, but we can never tire of hearing it because it is about lying and illusion and sincerity. I'm . . . now going to read you a text by . . . Jaime

Montestrela . . . a major Portuguese poet who lived in Brazil during the dictatorship . . . an extract from one of his books . . . *I Meet You*."

Her voice didn't waver. She did not look Antonio in the eye once. If she looked at me it was only fleetingly, but the name Montestrela aroused Irene's curiosity, and she whispered in my ear, "Is Montestrela that well known, then?"

Aurora plucked the strings of the violin to set a rhythm to her words.

"You have to read *I Meet You* as if it were an improvisation, the author . . . Jaime Montestrela . . . even indicates places where . . . where you have to stammer just like that so that listeners don't know whether they're already listening to *I Meet You* . . . It's a text about a man or rather a young woman who thinks she's met a man but all he did was spend some time with her and she's hurt by this because . . . one morning after he's slept at her house after they've made love no no no not made love those words don't belong here at all says Jaime Montestrela we have to be accurate and describe this openly because the young woman leads him over to her bed she gently takes his clothes off then undresses herself and there she is naked offered she gets on top of him she guides him and now yes we can say the words they make love it's still half dark but look the walls of the room are already being colored pink the sun is coming up over the city and the man wakes and looks at her she's sleeping naked on the white sheet she's so young her body's so firm so taut almost a child's body and something about her frightens him really frightens him it must because he gets out of bed that's right he doesn't stroke her doesn't kiss her doesn't even breathe in the smell of her hair no he gets up and dresses he has trouble tying his shoelaces and ridiculously he buttons his shirt too quickly and does it wrong and then he leaves he doesn't leave a note on the table he's never known what to say anyway he doesn't even drink a glass of water in the kitchen no he opens the door as quietly as he can and there he is outside like a thief he closes the door without a sound he goes down the stairs on tiptoe and runs away that's right he runs away the young woman knows this because no she was not sleeping no she stayed there motionless with her eyes closed and she heard his breathing his irritated groan about his uncooperative laces and when he was gone she walked over to the window and now she can see him running along the street and she understands yes yes yes he could have put down roots in her life like a lily on a pond who knows whether a water lily has roots or just floats on the water like Ophelia's corpse . . . but there it is, that man would never have been able to melt into her no no he lets everything slip through his fingers like sand and with each betrayal his world becomes as tiny as he is . . . but here at this point Montestrela uses the young woman's words he switches imperceptibly from *she* to *I* it's a pivotal moment . . ."

The crate wobbled slightly but, light-footed, Aurora immediately steadied herself . . . Young Karamazov couldn't take his eyes off her. He loved her of course. A guardian angel. Who was he? A childhood friend, an older brother, or younger, a faithful admirer? His inscrutable face expressed neither suffering nor resentment, barely even anxiety. He knew how tight a thread Aurora was balancing on, and yet was in no doubt it would hold fast.

"A pivotal switch from *she* to *I* yes but it is done very naturally because Montestrela is a fine workman when it comes to style a little too lyrical perhaps but you should be listening really it is the young woman talking she says what took you away from me you my prince of one luminous night you my Bohemian who wants none of eternity was it my overardent words intended to console you the inconsolable do you know that I wanted to run red through your veins like all the gold on earth do you know that I wanted to make pebbles burst into flower to reassure you to make you love me at last but I will not say anything no I will not say anything because I can feel my tears rising it's true I am made like that all it takes is a piece of music or a poem and there they are spilling out of me it's absolutely grotesque all this uncontrollable irrational emotion there was that poem that I read and reread twenty times I wanted to empty it of all my tears I wanted to rob it of all meaning but its intensity would not falter and yet it wasn't even the most beautiful of poems no it was just a needle wounding

my flesh so I thought never mind I shall love these tears
they're as much my strength as my weakness You are alive
they cry You you whose life has only just started but but
but shall I ever Lord God who does not exist shall I ever
exhaust my reservoir of tears shall I stop being moved by
anything but myself like old people who have not lived
enough Lord so I started drawing up a list of all the things
that can bring tears to my eyes until I realized it would be
endless but that does not matter Montestrela still launches
into this list and makes a note of everything and who cares
if some of it is clichéd he includes the fine dirty gray rain
that falls in autumn and the little girl playing hopscotch
the woman looking for traces of her youth in the mirror he
includes the little boy so proud to be on his father's shoulders and the woman weeping with rage at the gates of the
factory and the dead sparrow drying out on the ground
and the blue toy giraffe forgotten under the wardrobe and
more and more let's stop talking about Montestrela and
I Meet You and the young woman no no I am now going
to play the first movement of Sibelius's Violin Concerto
because it made me cry a lot."

Aurora took up her violin again and launched straight
into the piece. She played to perfection once again, showing just as much bravura and technique. And yet there was
something about her movements that surprised me, they
were expansive and supple, and I eventually realized that,
unusually, she was resting the violin on her right collar

bone, so that the strings were back to front. Aurora must have been transposing every move of the bow as, with her left hand very high in the air, she attacked the high notes with more resolve than ever. She finished the first movement and bravos rang out. She bowed twice, then stepped down from her Jaffa crate, put away her violin, and waved rather insistently at Karamazov. He hesitated, reluctant, but had to walk around the tables with his hat, which must never have housed a single coin in its felt existence. It was a good harvest, a lot of bills.

Irene wanted to give some money too. She rummaged through her bag, but the two young people slipped away without bringing the hat to our table. Fiddling automatically under the effect of his nerves, Antonio had strewn the tablecloth with dozens of tiny balls of bread. He didn't say a single word for the whole rest of the meal.

DAY SEVEN

■

*P*AUL

J dreamed of Irene and Manuela that night. A muddled hallucination in which Irene was taking a poodle called Extra for a walk through Lisbon. It started to snow and she opened an umbrella with an ornate handle shaped liked a toucan's beak. At this point Manuela appeared. She was wearing one of those Cretan dresses from the Minoan civilization, revealing firm breasts with imperious, erect nipples. She walked toward Irene, who was wearing the dog's collar around her neck but was meowing. A volcano then erupted in the middle of the Tagus (the reds and ochres of the image in my dream mimicked Turner's *Vesuvius in Eruption*). Gray ash covered the city, and I woke—in a sweat, confused by this unfathomable dream—to the sound of the telephone.

It was my brother Paul. The loan our father had taken out for the apartment on the rue Lecourbe had another eight years to run, and the bank's insurance company was refusing to cover for a suicide, since "the suicide of the insured party constitutes grounds for exclusion in the case of real estate." The company was asking us to reimburse the outstanding capital due "within twelve months" or to "take personal responsibility for continued monthly payments." The letterhead was familiar: it was from the bank to which our father had devoted his entire career. The management had sent a wreath for the funeral.

Paul had taken advice: in order to avoid the repayments, we needed a doctor's certificate stating that our father no longer "had all his mental faculties," and was not "conscious of the consequences of his act." But our father's doctor was refusing to testify to this. In his view Dad was in full possession of his senses and was not of a depressive disposition. Paul had gotten angry. So you could buy a rope from the do-it-yourself store in Courtenay, tie it to a beam, climb onto a Formica stool that you brought through from the kitchen, and slip your head into a running knot, all with a perfectly balanced mind. "Not all suicides are pathological," the doctor had kept saying. "Look at Romain Gary." The example had not struck Paul as persuasive.

To try to understand, Paul and I had read books on the subject. They stated that hangings are the work of the melancholic, that the act itself often takes place in the morning after a sleepless night spent mulling over morbid thoughts or pondering the recent loss of a loved one. But Mom had died more than eight years earlier. It could also involve the sudden redundancy of retirement. This was sometimes an explanation, but he had retired two years ago already. He had also met Laurence, a divorcée tackling her fifties with energy and fun, whom he had introduced to us and saw more and more regularly. In the church she had stared at the coffin and kept saying, "Why, but why?" and her eyes were sad and caring, but dry.

It was a religious funeral. An initiative of Uncle Simon's, he took care of everything. Dad was not a believer, perhaps even something of a blasphemer, but his brother believed in the cathartic value of rituals, in ceremonies, and tradition. In his sermon, the priest talked about "great sorrow" and said we must "not despair of eternal salvation for a man who has died by his own hand. By means known only to Himself, God would grant him repentance. Let us pray for Jacques, who took his own life. Praise the Lord." No one repeated the words "Praise the lord," as they are supposed to, but after waiting for a moment, the priest carried on as if nothing untoward had happened.

Thinking of those empty pronouncements reminded me of one of Montestrela's tales that I had just translated:

The people of the Adjiji archipelago are convinced that God, whom they call Niaka, is very evil and that the

Devil, whom they call Puku, is good. They follow the moral codes decreed by Puku's prophets, exhorting them to renounce Niaka. When all is said and done, this does not change much.

At one point during the service Uncle Simon leaned over to us and tilted his chin toward the back of the nave. A rather chubby woman with permed blond hair and a veil was hanging back, standing beside a pillar, clutching an embroidered handkerchief. We didn't know her: could this be "Solange"? Dad had once admitted to Simon that he had a mistress, a client from his bank branch, a "very beautiful woman" (those were his words) who was also married. Their relationship began in the safety deposit room, under neon lights, surrounded by locked drawers, a setting that made their liaison all the more unimaginable. According to Simon, she and Dad were still seeing each other even when our mother had to go into the hospital. They had broken off all contact after her death, as if, with Mom dead, it was now impossible for Dad to be unfaithful to her. It must have been Solange: she left very quickly, without saying hello to anyone.

The police inquiry had retraced what Dad did on his last day. He must have caught the 10:15 train to Courtenay and the bus to Montcardon, sitting at the back, as he always did, then walked to his little house on the rue du Mail. There he set up his incident in the barn, a cinder-block building attached to a windowless wall. But beforehand he had had lunch in the local restaurant. The owner hadn't noticed anything unusual. Dad had the dish of the day, mushroom lasagna, drank a glass of Côtes du Rhône, and had a decaf coffee. It was this decaf that most surprised the inspector. Our father's doctor had warned him to avoid caffeine, but what difference would it make on a day like that? Perhaps he wasn't yet thinking about dying. Or had simply developed a taste for decaf.

Dad left no letter, nothing that explained anything. Paul and I searched through the house. Nothing. I resented him for that, I still do. I'd have been happier if he had left with a declaration of paternal love, the only one he would ever have made to us. A sort of absolution for having failed to see or notice anything. A few tender sentences we could have clung to while the coffin was being lowered into the ground. I spent many nights dreaming of that letter. It would have to start with the words "My sons, my dear sons . . . ," and I didn't really give a damn about the rest. But Dad had always been the silent type, and it was a bit late now for him to change.

He must have lain down in his first-floor bedroom, the bedspread was still crumpled. He had taken out a few yellowed books—or perhaps they just hadn't been put away. I had never known him to read those books, but I couldn't see what to make of them. Still, I did note down the titles, as if they held some impenetrable secret: Mallarmé's *Verse and Prose*, the Teubner edition of the *Odyssey*, Jules Verne's *Voyage to the Center of the Earth*, and an old 1898 edition of Leon Bloy's *The Ungrateful Beggar*. Its epigraph was a quote from Barbey d'Aurevilly: "The most beautiful names borne by men were the names given by their enemies."

Dad had forgotten to close the iron gate, as well as the door to the barn. Unless he had actually left them open deliberately so that someone would notice, would think there had been a burglary. That was what happened. A neighbor found his body the same day, shortly before nightfall. The pathologist had set the time of death at about four in the afternoon.

No, the insurance would not pay, and Lecourbe would bring in a lot less than anticipated. Paul also suggested dropping the price of Montcardon, to close the deal swiftly, and to give it to an estate agent's office in Paris. I agreed: of course, the agents in Courtenay weren't going around telling prospective buyers that the previous owner had hanged himself in the barn, but the facts always came out in the end, and the sale had already fallen through three times.

Paul said a few more words about what an idiot our father's doctor was and the elegance of the bank's last gesture, and we hung up.

Paul wanted to sort everything out as quickly as possible. It was his way of running away, of hurrying through grief. Back when our mother died, he had set up house in

Milan for no apparent reason. He found work in an architect's office, pitching up for a few days every Christmas with a big panettone and some Asti Spumante. His exile lasted three years, then he came back to France. Once the inheritance had been carved up, I knew he would go away again, and that we would gradually become what we had always been to each other, although we never admitted it: strangers. I thought he would get back in touch with me when his children were born, when he had them. I hadn't imagined for one moment that I myself might be a father.

I felt like calling Paul back, telling him what a family *could* be like, or just two brothers. Telling him about the affection I felt for him, for my younger brother who had been too many years younger for me for a long time, whom I got to know so little and so badly, also telling him how hard it would be for me to lose the scraps I had left of my childhood. I didn't do it. I thought of writing to him. I didn't do that either.

I HAD A shower and went down to the cafe to read the *Diário*. It devoted most of page 3 to a long article about Pinheiro's bronze coat of mail. This style of armor was a perfect copy of the *lorica hamata* that Roman legionaries took from the Celts and wore for six centuries. It was made of linked rings: each ring was connected to four others and sealed with a rivet known as a barleycorn, and this was illustrated with a detailed diagram. The rings were flattened and had a diameter of just a few millimeters, so the coat of mail comprised several hundred thousand of them. A peculiar detail: some of the rings had been soldered to wires connected to 4.5-volt batteries, as in toning belts athletes used for their abdominal muscles. The setup was absurd, though, given that bronze is a very good conductor so the power would inevitably be dissipated in short circuits.

The *Diário*'s journalist had had an identical one made by a locksmith, who was kept busy for a whole week with the task. The alloy used was not commercially available, and he had had to order it from a foundry because no bronze sculpture had so much copper and so little pewter in it: there was also some arsenic which made the alloy harder, making the article more clean-cut. As he reproduced the original, the craftsman became convinced that Pinheiro's coat of mail had been one of a limited edition of "at least half a dozen."

For nearly three hours the journalist had worn the hat, bronze bangles, and chain mail, right next to his skin as Pinheiro had, although legionaries never actually wore it naked like this but over a linen shirt. Once the wires were connected to batteries, the experiment had become painful, far less because of the electrical current than because his body hair kept getting caught in the rings.

I covered all of this in my article, bolstering it with a few details on the capture of Rome by the Gauls under Brennus, to whom minor history owes the story of the geese at the Capitol—and to whom Roman military history owes this form of chain mail.

My brother Paul was given a Vercingetorix the Gaul outfit for his sixth birthday. A winged helmet as on cigarette packets, a brown cape in rough fabric, a wide sword, a round shield, and a plastic coat of mail. It was a family celebration, in the countryside at Montcardon. I was thirteen and bored, rereading old Tarzan and Bob Morane stories in our bedroom. My brother spent the day running all over the place in his Gallic chieftain's costume; toward nightfall he wanted to go and play in the woods. My mother asked me to take him and play with him. I dug my heels in and she reprimanded me with a frown: "Vincent—it's your brother's birthday."

I sighed and went out with Paul.

We simply had to follow a dirt track alongside the house. It was impracticable by bicycle because it was too rutted up by tractor tires. First we had to walk past two cornfields, then a vineyard, and you reached the woods after half a mile. You went into the woods on a path edged with ivy and brambles, cutting through an embankment. It was just a few dozen hectares of straggly, poorly maintained forest, but in springtime there were hundreds of daffodils under the trees, and even lily of the valley. My brother liked going for walks there, bringing home moss, collecting gleaming blue beetles in jars where they scuttled under damp tree bark. Down below us, in the light of the setting sun, was the watercourse, the Vougre, where people swam in summer, although it was barely deeper than a brook. Nearby were the dark waters of a pond, known as the Tramen Pond, where people went boating. My brother could lie in the grass on the banks for hours watching the balletic moves of yellow-bellied newts, but never daring to catch them. In the middle of the forest there was also a dead tree with black, clawlike branches, the Devil Tree. It terrified Paul and that was my fault: I was the one who called it that, and I had told my little brother terrible stories, full of witches and monsters. When the tree appeared around a bend on a walk, Paul would run and hide behind me, scared. I protected him from the demon with incantations and curses. Paul's disillusion when he grew up was in direct proportion to the admiration he had once felt.

I'll never forget that afternoon. Paul is running ahead of me, pushing aside brambles with his shield. From time to time he strays from the path, pursuing one of the pond's big green dragonflies with his sword. Then he comes back, laughing, victorious. I've brought a comic book with me and don't pay much attention to him. At some point I can't hear him anymore. I call him. He doesn't answer. I shout his name again several times and, succumbing to genuine fear, start running toward the pond. He isn't there. I run to the river, climb back up the bank yelling Paul, Paul, with all my strength, all the way to a backwater of the Vougre even though he can't have had time to get there. I go back to the Tramen, I search through the reeds, wading out into the water, I daren't think the unimaginable, of finding a little blond-haired Gallic chieftain floating in the water, drowned in his chain mail, still wearing his helmet. I even go to the Devil Tree. Maybe Paul's overcome his fear, maybe he's waiting for me there, sitting on a low branch? But no. It's getting dark. I can see less and less clearly. I stand with my back against a tree and start to cry. I'm paralyzed with guilt, and I'm also frightened of my mother's fury, but I must go home and ask for help. I run along the path in sodden shoes. Again and again I trip in the deep ruts gouged out by farm machinery, grazing my knees and elbows and hands.

I barge through the door to the house and see Paul in the kitchen. He got hungry, wanted a jelly sandwich, looked for me for a while in the woods and, when he didn't find me, came home on his own. My mother sees me in the doorway, dripping and filthy. She comes toward me, beside herself with rage and, unable to articulate a sentence, she slaps me to dispel her own anxiety. I don't try to avoid the blow, one of the very few in my life. The pain in my cheek frees me from my own tension, tears well up immediately and I go to our room and throw myself on my bed. I sob uncontrollably. I know that that could have been the day when my life turned upside down, when I would have been burdened forever with the atrocity of Paul's memory. I imagine the nightmare of a life without Paul, a shameful life that would have to be lived in the shadow of his death, and yet, somewhere in that total darkness, in that abyss of misery, there is a vertiginous sort of appeal, as if I knew that only a glow as dark as that could give meaning to my own life, as if you had to be infinitely guilty to be truly saved.

I put down the *Diário* with its pictures of chain mail and drove away the images it had evoked. I went over to the hotel. Antonio had left a note for me with the porter.

"It's early. I called your place, but you weren't there. I'm going to the Estufa Fria. I need to talk to Aurora, to explain. Then I'm going to take some pictures around Belém, I'll be gone all day. Let's meet up this evening, if you can. Irene's still asleep. Tell her I'll be back at about five. You'll think of an explanation, I know you'll be discreet. Thanks. A."

I didn't have to wait for Irene, she was having her breakfast. I found an explanation, and was also discreet.

I said I was meeting someone. No, I couldn't have lunch with her, or meet for coffee in the afternoon, and I probably wouldn't be around this evening either. But tomorrow, it's a promise. I stood up, pleased with my indifference. She looked at me as if she thought I was going to hurt her and she couldn't give a damn.

IT WAS ALSO the first day of the Pinheiro trial. I could have waited for the reports in the Portuguese press, but I had an official pass after all, and I was curious to see how he behaved in court.

The courtroom was packed, the press box heaving. Pinheiro seemed half asleep in the dock, utterly silent, his eyes blank. That morning they were giving an inventory of the murders. He had confessed to the police for all those that involved the Luger, but his lawyer made much of reminding the jury that, for three of these, he had a cast-iron alibi. The same weapon must, therefore, have been used by several assassins. That would be the position taken by the defense: Pinheiro, who had accepted the blame for all the murders, could in fact be innocent of them all, and why not also the last one, if the culprit had dropped the firearm in his pocket. Then he would simply have been the accomplice responsible for disposing of the gun, in a strange complex mechanism.

They then showed some images provided by the pathologist. They were poorly framed, workaday shots, showing blood-stained bodies frozen in death, captured on film out of respect for protocol, without humanity. This obscenity created an awkward tension among people in the public gallery, but Pinheiro didn't look at them.

I was just leaving the courtroom, feeling slightly nauseous, when Pinheiro stood up and started shouting: "Why are you degrading Heaven and Earth? Why are you pointlessly humiliating the children of men? Why charge the twinkling stars with your futile laws? Why, when we are born free, do you make us slaves of an inanimate heaven?"

Then he sat back down, dazed by so many words. His lawyer, disconcerted, leaned toward him and seemed to give copious advice. Pinheiro's head dropped forward as if he had fallen asleep. As I was leaving, the policeman next to me muttered, "What an idiot."

The cop looked stupid too. Which detracted nothing from the accuracy of his comment.

AT ONE O'CLOCK I was at the Brasileira. I had lunch there, spinning out each course, hoping Manuela would come by. I liked the newfound fever that was gradually driving out my longing for Irene. But at three o'clock she still wasn't there.

I went home to my studio and worked on a few more *Contos aquosos*, whose title I had decided to translate as *Liquid Tales* because *Aqueous Tales* sounded too much like "queer tales." And "liquid" had the advantage of evoking the absurd, playful way Montestrela liquidated great philosophical themes:

On the planet FH76, the bodies of living beings are not fused to their spirits. This means that the spirit can sometimes die long before the body. The latter carries on eating, running, conversing, or even copulating to the death. Bodily activity can continue for several years without anyone noticing a thing.

Finding an editor for *Liquid Tales* would have been sensible, but I was beginning to feel, like Gertrude Stein, "If it can be done, why do it?" I was afraid that, as soon as an agreement was reached, I would be far less motivated. I was translating the four hundred and third tale when there was a knock at my door.

It was Custódia. He had climbed the three floors slowly but was flushed and out of breath.

"I was just checking you're here," he said, raising his hat. "And, anyway, the shelves are too heavy for me to bring them up on my own. Where are they to go?"

I asked him in and showed him the wall. The drawing of Duck was there, framed, beneath the window. But he didn't look at it. He just tapped the wall with a finger and listened to its resonance.

"We could hang it off the ground here, if you like. It's a weight-bearing wall and it would hold up well. It would look better and keep the floor space clear. I made it with brackets and I've brought my drill."

I nodded and we went downstairs. I was behind Custódia; he was losing his hair and his bald patch revealed the
first liver spots. He was probably not yet sixty but was as
worn as his gray cardigan. A nasty man, a brute even, was
what his neighbor Pita had said. I just felt sorry for him.

We unloaded the frame from the truck, it was incredibly heavy. Custódia handed me some gloves.

"Oh yes, it's definitely not balsa wood. We'll take the
shelves up separately."

We took a rest on each landing and when we reached
my studio, I went in first and saw the portrait of Duck. I
was suddenly terribly ashamed of stooping so low, being
so abject. I flipped the picture to face the wall, to hide his
daughter's face from Custódia. I didn't want to produce
such pointless pain. It didn't matter anymore.

We put the frame against the wall, went down for the
shelves, and came straight back up without exchanging a
word. Custódia marked out the screw holes with a pencil.
Then he moved the frame a few inches to one side to get to
a socket, drilled deep into the wall, and inserted the pegs.
I held the shelf unit and he secured it with a few turns of
the screwdriver. The result wasn't at all bad. Custódia had
added a frieze and some moldings, filled the joints with
wood glue, and waxed the unit. Moments later we had put
the shelves in.

"Your books?" Custódia asked. "Shall we put them in to
see what it looks like?"

"I—I don't have any. In a trunk, somewhere else. I'll bring them over."

Custódia pulled on the cord of his drill and that was when he caught the portrait. It fell onto the tiled floor and the glass broke. Custódia swore and apologized.

"I'll mend it," he said, "don't you worry about it."

Before I had a chance to react he was assessing the damage, turning the frame over in his hand. He looked at the portrait for a long time, then leaned it back against the wall.

"I'm sorry."

"It's just glass, really."

"I mean forgive me for looking at the picture for so long. She looks so like my daughter."

Custódia nodded, it was impossible to know what he was thinking, and all at once I was afraid Duck might be dead. It was this fear rather than deceitfulness that made me ask, "Your daughter?"

"Yes."

"How—how old is she?" I persisted, hoping for reassurance.

"Twenty-seven. Is it someone you know, the woman in the picture, or did you buy it just like that?"

"She's . . . a friend. I drew it." And to prove the point I showed him the charcoal still lying on my desk. Custódia put away his tools. I felt fate had decided for me, and I didn't have the right to let the opportunity go.

"And . . . do you have grandchildren?"

"Two. A boy and a little girl."

Custódia stood up with a sigh and dusted himself off.

"How old are they?"

"The boy's eleven and the girl's six, I think. I'm not sure. I hardly ever see them. It's not easy, nowadays, a father-daughter relationship."

"Tell me. She doesn't have a red Fiat, does she? I saw a woman who looked liked this picture in a red Fiat."

"I wouldn't know. Honestly, we don't see each other much. Not much at all. That's the way it is."

He picked up his gloves and tools and opened the door. He threw a last long glance at the portrait of Duck.

"It's incredible," he said. "It really is her, believe me. Actually, she works quite near here. Printers on the corner of the rua da Barroca."

He shook my hand, his was callused, rough, he could easily have broken my fingers, but the handshake was civil. I closed the door and gathered up the broken glass. Custódia's truck set off noisily.

Printers, on the corner of the rua da Barroca, who'd have thought it?

I remembered a story that I knew to be true, the one about a Jew who survived the Nazi camps where he lost his entire family, who emigrated to the United States and settled in Brooklyn, gradually rebuilding his shattered life. Then one day he scratched a car in the parking lot of

the supermarket he went to every week. The driver was
his own wife, who he thought had died. She'd been living
five blocks from him for twenty years.

On the corner of the rua da Barroca. It was so simple.

I SET OFF in search of the printers and found it in a matter of minutes. It was called LisboPrint, Soares & Filhos.
The metal shutter was closed. The company offered faxing and photocopying services, and the window display
showed business cards, wedding invitations, and small
bespoke pieces such as posters and leaflets. I ate not far
from there, not as impatient to get to the next day as I
would have thought.

Then I went back to my studio and opened my black
notebook for *The Clearing* and turned on my Mac to copy
out the latest sentences. It wasn't any good. I wanted to
rewrite the whole text, to put it into first-person narra-
tive, like a private journal, to turn it into Pescheux's inner
monologue, a rambling discourse, occasionally tinged with
a lyricism that I wanted to ruffle up. I tried out the effect
on the first few pages: "Met Galois at Palais-Royal. He was
kissing Stéphanie and didn't see me. My whole being was
instantly reduced to images. The traitress's smile betrayed
the feverishness of their every move, hidden moisture,

flesh and sweat, it pierced through me till I felt nauseous, till I flinched, I pulled myself together, ran toward them, drunk with rage . . ."

That wasn't very good either. I gave up.

It was late already. The radio was talking about a terrible earthquake in Mexico City, 8.2 on the Richter scale. The city was in ruins, emergency services were converging. I listened for a while, and put my few books, including *Contos aquosos*, onto Custódia's shelves. Then I turned out the light but didn't draw the curtains. I couldn't get to sleep. Someone rang my doorbell: Antonio. I turned on a lamp but the light was too harsh for him, so we stayed there in shadow with just the glow from the street. The facade of the building opposite went from green to red, red to green, with the traffic lights at the crossroads.

Antonio asked for a drink. I put two glasses on the table and an almost empty bottle of ouzo. I opened the fridge to get a jug of chilled water, and closed it quickly so its wan light didn't compromise the mood of trust. Tonio's forehead was gleaming with clammy, anxious sweat. I wished he would wipe it, because I couldn't take my eyes off that almost phosphorescent strip of skin reflecting colors on the street like a wet sidewalk. Orange, then red, back to green.

He didn't say anything for a long time. I could see he was shaking but his eyes were obscured by shadows. He was breathing hard, or perhaps that was merely the rarefied, obsessive awareness of sound produced by the dark.

"Do you want to sleep?" he asked.

"It doesn't matter."

I was ashamed for not trying to disguise how tired I was. Red, green, a motorbike setting off and fading away. He sighed.

"Row with Irene. Violent. Nasty. In the letter I called her 'sweet.' Anyway . . . she's leaving tomorrow."

"Did you see Aurora?"

He whispered her name as if calling to her softly.

"I went to the hothouse, to her 'island,' as she calls it. She was there with a fair-haired man with very fine, almost feminine features, he was holding her hand, they were kissing. As soon as she saw me she came over, smiling. She didn't seem to feel caught out. I wanted to explain things but she stopped me short by kissing my cheek. She introduced me to her friend, with a simple 'Timoteo, my friend.' And to him she said, 'Antonio.' She didn't say anything resentful, behaved quite naturally, was sweet. It was as if an eternity had passed. I belonged to her past. I left pretty much right away. I looked back one last time, Aurora and her Timoteo gave me a friendly wave goodbye. And I knew I'd lost her."

He put his glass on the table, near the Macintosh.

"Do you think she really loved me?"

I repressed a smile at this adolescent question. But what sort of answer could I give, as I know nothing about love, and never understand women better than on the day they leave me. He leaned with his back to the wall, against the nearly empty bookshelves. We stayed like that for a long time, not speaking.

I recognized the color of that silence. Years ago I spent three weeks in Inuit country, in Iqaluit and then Kugaaruk, far above the Arctic Circle. That was where I got the Reverend Samuel Wallis's mask. Rather than staying in the Pelly Bay Inn, a hotel made of prefabricated units, I rented a room in a private home. My host was called Niam Amgoalik. In Inupiak, Niam means "sweetness" or "my darling" but, although he was welcoming enough, this man was not the image Europeans have of sweetness. One evening when Niam and I were in the living room—I was reading a copy of *Nunatsiak News* several months old and he was repairing the handlebar of his Skidoo—there was a knock at the door and a man came straight in without waiting for an answer. Niam didn't say a word, just gave a friendly nod. The visitor took a Coke from his bag, opened it and sat slowly in an armchair. Niam carried on mending his handlebars while his friend sipped his Coke. It wasn't completely silent: Niam breathed loudly as he tinkered with the brake lever, his friend burped from time to time, and I turned the pages of the newspaper. Outside there was the noise of a snowstorm, the smack of a badly secured shutter.

I eventually got used to this muteness and forgot my initial embarrassment. But while Niam and his friend were sharing the simple fact of being together, I was withdrawing into myself to the point of indifference. And when, after half an hour, or perhaps a little more, the friend waved goodbye to Niam and left, I felt incomplete, like a deaf person who has watched musicians play but heard nothing of the tune. I never knew Niam's friend's name.

A motorbike backfiring on the street broke the spell. Antonio knocked back the rest of his ouzo.

"Thanks, Vincent. I'll go back to the hotel."

But he didn't move. The wall turned from red to green. I went over to the window and opened it wide, a breeze carrying the smell of the sea swept through the room.

"I think I have a couple beers, if you like."

"Okay."

I opened the fridge, and as I took the bottles out the cold neon light briefly illuminated the portrait of Duck. It was too late to hide it from Antonio.

"What the hell's that, Vincent? It's—it can't be."

He took out his wallet, searching through it feverishly.

"Yes, it's Duck," I preempted him. "I—drew it from memory. I thought she was beautiful. Her face is so . . . pure."

Antonio found the photo and compared it to the portrait, speechless.

"I know I should have told you," I went on, "but I never thought you'd end up seeing it."

"But, Vincent, I don't understand. You don't know her, and this portrait . . . it's not just a drawing."

"I could give it to you, it doesn't mean anything. It's just a, what would you call it? Just an amateur sketch. I wanted to get back into working with charcoal. Since meeting Aurora."

"You're messing with me, Vincent . . . I think this is . . . sick. Kind of love by proxy."

"What are you talking about? What love? Forgive the comparison, but Leonardo da Vinci wasn't in love with Mona Lisa. It's just a picture."

I must have hit the right note because Antonio grimaced, then smiled properly.

"Okay. I'll give you that. I should apologize. Let's open these bottles."

I prized the lids off and Antonio took one of the beers and walked over to the window. He looked at the portrait, more relaxed, appeased.

"It's good, for something done from memory. It would have been even more faithful if you'd had the photo. You've aged her a bit, but she must actually look like that now."

I didn't mention the printers on the rua da Barroca but asked, "Wouldn't you like to know?"

"No."

It was a cold no. I showed Antonio the map of the Okavango Delta.

"Do you remember Okavango in Botswana, Antonio? You took the pictures, I wrote the piece. You hired a

small plane, flew over the delta and the Moremi Reserve
. . . They were magnificent pictures."

"That was a long time ago. I don't know why you brought
that up. Sorry, I'm tired, I'm going back."

Antonio finished his beer, nodded, and left.

But no one forgets the Okavango. It's an African river,
a really long river, much more powerful than the Tagus
or the Rhône and over half a mile wide at the Popa Falls.
Its source is in Angola, it flows through Namibia before
reaching Botswana. That's where it meets the Kalahari
Desert, where it coils into meanders, creating a rich tropical forest and producing a vast, swampy, saltwater delta
that is home to tens of thousands of flamingoes. In the
dry season, there are a myriad of islands formed around
giant termite mounds and dense shrubs. Tourist leaflets describe luxuriant marshes, a miracle performed by
water, an earthly paradise. All rivers run into the sea, yet
the sea is not full, says Ecclesiastes. That's not true: the
Kalahari is vast and all the water of the Okavango gradually evaporates, or seeps into mud and sand.

The Okavango never reaches the sea. Its destiny as a
river is never fulfilled. Of course other watercourses have
the same fate: the Awash in the Afar region of Ethiopia
simply irrigates that country's great lakes, the Bear River
ends its days in the brine of the Great Salt Lake. But no
river is as powerful as the Okavango, none as indomitable.
Its defeat in the face of the scorching Kalahari Desert is a

catastrophe, its slow absorption like the end of the world. I've always liked old geographical maps, which is why I had bought the one I hung on the wall. That old map of the Okavango Basin was a metaphor for unfinished business, for adversity, for an unreachable goal.

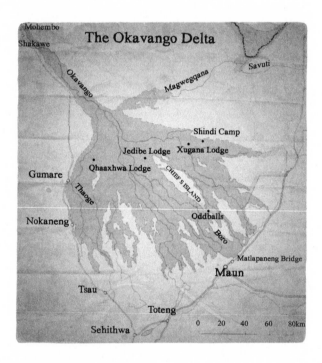

I listened to Antonio walking along the deserted street. He suddenly started running and I heard the sound of his racing footsteps for a long time. Then the hubbub from farther down in the city smothered everything. I knew why

Antonio was running. Sometimes the sound of our own footsteps becomes unbearable. It describes our impotence, our density, our weight. Walking means being resigned to that. So we refuse to be, and we run, it doesn't matter where, because we're running away from ourselves.

DAY EIGHT

Duck

*J*n the morning I bought the *Diário*. The front page showed Mexico City in ruins, buildings collapsed like houses of cards, rows of bodies, and the dust-caked faces of survivors. There too, churches had caved in onto the faithful. On an inside page was the report on the Pinheiro case. The journalist who had covered it had some literary background. In Pinheiro's incoherent outburst he had recognized Petrarch's criticism of astrologers and their predictions. So he didn't like horoscopes then. What to make of that? You tell me.

I hadn't envisaged the Pinheiro case like this. I had hoped—and the general public had hoped to an even greater extent—there would be confessions, or better, revelations. Diabolical machinations revealed for all to see. I'd pictured a sect, a clandestine criminal hierarchy with esoteric rites. But everything was still dark and vague, and I was almost ashamed of sending the newspaper my daily chatty report of this obscurity.

It was not until eleven o'clock that I made up my mind to go to LisboPrint, Soares & Filhos printers, with the excuse of photocopying and faxing my article. I felt, with a hint of superstition, that fate would repay me for my efforts to curb my eagerness. I was hoping to see Duck, but the premises went back a long way, and a wide set of shelves housing files blocked my view of the presses and any employees. The only person at the till was a tall man of about forty with an overly purple tie. He was a bit slow and clumsy: the photocopier wasn't self-service, neither was the fax, and it took him nearly ten minutes to complete these tasks.

I tried to find an excuse to stay a little longer, to get a chance to see her. I thought about business cards, which people kept asking me for. The tall guy shouted *Constantino!* in a loud high-pitched voice, several times, until a pudgy little man built like Ubu appeared. He took out three large files filled with samples of hundreds of different styles.

"You've certainly come to the right place for business cards: what with the size, choice of paper, font, layout, and inking techniques, we can give you the choice of, guess how many combinations. Guess."

"I—I don't know."

"Okay, ten sizes, twenty types of paper, fifteen fonts, ten basic formats, and six different inking methods, that gives us . . . a hundred and eighty thousand different business cards! And that's not counting logos and colored ink," he concluded triumphantly.

"And can you give me a recommendation?"

He pointed to the first card on the first page of the first file.

"Take the standard one. It's sensible and professional, it's simple without being boring. How many do you need? I would recommend two hundred. It's not much more expensive to print than one hundred, and with five hundred you never use them all. If you did need more, don't worry, we keep the offset plates for a year."

"All right then, two hundred of the standard style."

"Perfect. It's our best seller. You'll be very pleased with it."

I paid for the photocopying and the cards. It was no giveaway. I'd now run out of ideas so I just came out and asked, "Forgive me, but I came by a few days ago and was served by a dark-haired young woman who—"

"Oh, are you also picking up a rebound book? You should have said. When did you leave it with us? If it was last week and it was being leather-bound, it's a bit too soon. They haven't been delivered."

I immediately thought of the *Contos aquosos* that I had in my pocket.

"No, it's something I want to have done, I have the book with me."

The man called Constantino cried *Cátia!* two or three times, with the same energy and the same high-pitched voice as the photocopying man. It must have been the exact intonation and volume needed for a voice to carry over the noise of the machines.

Cátia . . . so this wasn't Duck. I was disappointed, but it was logical: old Custódia saw so little of his daughter that he probably didn't know where she now worked. I would have to start all over again. At least I would have some business cards to hand out.

But a young woman appeared and there she was. She had changed very little, perhaps her features had hollowed slightly. Her straight hair was cut shorter, under her work smock she was wearing jeans and a T-shirt. She was a modern young woman, ordinarily pretty and prettily ordinary. I thought I would be disconcerted, bowled over when my secret heroine of the last few days turned up. But I felt the tension in me subside, I was finally liberated by the very simplicity of her incarnation.

I must have looked slightly dazed. She peered at me probingly, tilting her head. I had forgotten what I was doing there.

"This *is* for a book binding, isn't it?" she asked.

She had a slightly hoarse, deep, but very sensual voice that I would never have suspected from her. I showed her my copy of the *Contos*. She opened it and examined the inner pages. She was a professional.

"Apart from the cover, it's in good condition. It's got, let me see, twelve signatures. I'll redo all the stitching and put a double lining on the spine. Will these be all right, this marbled paper for the cover, and this green for the cloth-bound spine and the corners?"

"Green, yes, that would be great."

"That's good then. I'll be able to slip it in with another order right away today. Not only will it cost you less, but you'll have it back in under forty-eight hours, perhaps even tomorrow. Glue dries quickly at the moment. Would you like the bookmark in red, blue, or gold?"

"Whatever you like."

"Let's say gold. It'll look very nice with the green cloth binding."

She handed me her card: Cátia Moniz. I smiled—hers was also the standard style, Constantino's best seller.

"Call me tomorrow morning then, Mr. . . ."

"Balmer. Vincent Balmer. I've given all my contact details . . . for my cards."

Before taking the book she looked at its cover.

"Jaime Montestrela . . ."

"Do you know him? You're definitely the first."

"He wrote a beautiful book, *Cidade de lama*, about the loneliness of exile. I haven't read it, but the phrase 'exile is an endless insomnia' is from him."

CÁTIA MONIZ. CÁTIA Moniz. Nothing of the Duck I had imagined could be filed under that completely new name.

When I reached Rossio Square it started pouring rain. I sheltered and watched the slow pirouette of taxis describing a wide circle around Dom Pedro IV's column. It was 1985 but the Peugeot 403 was already looking ancient. It was closely followed by a Datsun with a crumpled front wing, then a Mercedes with battered chrome that was spewing as much soot as smoke.

A young couple were waiting at the head of the queue, more mismatched than a pelican and a chickadee. He was tall and bulky but trussed up in a tight raincoat, his neck squeezed by a too-thin tie, she was short and slim, wearing a soaked multicolored dress. From that far away, hidden as she was by a straw hat ravaged by the rain shower, she could have been Aurora, Manuela, or even Duck. Watching them, I succumbed to the all-encompassing amazement I always feel about lives that are not my own. The boy talked the whole time while she gazed into the distance. When the 403 stopped beside them, she opened the rear door, climbed in quickly, and leaned toward the driver. Her movements suggested relief, she was in a hurry for the date to be over. She closed the door and the young man stayed outside, mouth agape, his words hanging in the air.

He leaned forward, almost kneeling, and gesticulated for her to lower the window, to exchange a last few words or perhaps a kiss. She looked away and the Peugeot plowed its tires into an oily puddle as it set off. The young man in the tie watched the Peugeot move away before climbing into the Datsun behind. He closed the door on his raincoat, a big flap of it hung down to the ground and was spattered with mud as the taxi pulled away. The city displayed two or three hundred shows like this in parallel, comedies and tragedies, and I didn't know what to make of this gift of fate.

The shower stopped, the sun dried the sidewalks, and I walked to the Brasileira. I wanted to see Manuela. In the previous night's unfathomable nightmare she was the one I wanted. And perhaps that was all I needed to understand from that dream. That one fantasy was coming to an end, given that I was ready—at worst—to move on to another. If she hadn't been there I would have kept on walking to the theater and demanded to see her. But she was at the Brasileira, sitting at a table with a woman with very short blond hair, an elegant, athletic woman, a little older than she was. Manuela was not wearing her provocative corset, just a dress that could have been demure if she hadn't shortened it by pulling it up over a belt.

I waved to her and she introduced us: Anna, Vincent. The woman looked up at me and, with her cool reception, implied I was interrupting. I waited at another table and ordered a coffee. The blond woman looked annoyed, she squeezed Manuela's hand and stood up, and Manuela sat still for a moment before giving me a little wave. I went to join her.

"I'm sorry, Vincent. Anna's not very sociable. How's the dragon Irene doing?"

"She's—she's fine."

Manuela laughed. "I meant you and her."

"I'm—I'm getting better."

"Well, that's reassuring. I didn't see much of her, but I can tell you what does it for her, she's desperate to be found attractive and terrified of being abandoned. She must have given you quite a runaround."

"Because that was what I wanted."

"Of course. When someone looks like a whipped dog, you want to hurt them. It's the rule."

"Do I look like a whipped dog?"

"With her you do. You look like you've lost before you've even tried. No one wants to be with a permanent loser."

I looked at the dolphin on her wrist and felt like touching her hand. I took her fingers for a moment but she withdrew them immediately.

"Vincent . . . please. Don't always put yourself in situations where you can be humiliated. Do you really misread things that badly?"

"I—I'm really sorry."

"And stop apologizing the whole time. There's nothing tragic about all this. You don't know anything about me,

I'll tell you a bit. As you're looking at the dolphin, I'll tell you about that. You have to go back seventeen years, during the Angolan war. Portugal sent tens of thousands of soldiers out there, more even, and in among all those young conscripts was Francisco, my father's best friend's son. But Francisco had hardly landed before he was killed by a grenade, deep in the jungle, in an ambush near Luanda. His body was repatriated, and our whole family went to his funeral. It was snowing that day, that's rare here but it was January. We all filed past the hole in the ground, to throw in a red carnation. The engraving on the marble gravestone read "1948–1968," and when I saw those two dates, I started shaking and crying. I didn't know Francisco, I'd never even met him, but I just couldn't stop. A girl came over to me and took my hand, she cried with me. She was a cousin of Francisco's, Delfina, she was just sixteen, almost the same age as me, she didn't know anything about me, but thought I must be Francisco's girlfriend. She didn't let go of my hand for the whole ceremony. When we had to head back to Lisbon we quickly exchanged addresses and phone numbers and promised to meet up. We both already knew that we were in love. Yes, don't look at me like that, Vincent, the great love of my teenage years was called Delfina. She was from a military family and went to school at the Instituto de Odivelas, a very strict, very Catholic boarding school with the motto Thought, Courage and Devotion. We had to hide. In 1962 when they wanted to put one of the leaders of the Communist Party in prison, they used the excuse that he was homosexual. The Odivelas district was a really long way from where I lived, but every evening I used to take the Eléctrico M, and then a bus, and I would meet Delfina in the Instituto's old chapel, which had one door that didn't lock properly. Sometimes we could even stay there all night, hiding in the refectory. One night, another girl gave Delfina away, and we were caught. The insults were appalling, there were physical blows, I was hounded out, the Mother Superior dragged Delfina up to her room by her hair, Delfina screaming, calling me to help her. I don't know what happened after that but that night Delfina fell from the third floor. 'She walked on the roof and slipped' was the story given by the management, who never mentioned the earlier scene to her family. A tragic accident. But it wasn't true. Delfina had also slit her wrists with a razor, I discovered that later. I can tell you what happened. They beat her, insulted her, belittled her, and humiliated her to the point where she slit her wrists and threw herself out of the window. Or maybe they even pushed her out to disguise her suicide. I went to see her father to tell him everything, and he was horrible too. His daughter couldn't have been a lesbian, it was unthinkable, in fact he couldn't even say the word. I wasn't allowed to go to Delfina's funeral. The following day, I went to my love's grave with my sister who knew everything and hadn't left my side since Delfina died because she was so frightened

I would kill myself too. There were flowers everywhere, and even a bouquet of white roses from the Instituto de Odivelas, I spat on it and threw it as far as I could, and I screamed like an animal in that cemetery. Then I sang a song by Antonio Botto, you might know it, Delfina really liked his work. I can still remember it:

Envolve-me amorosamente
Na cadeia de teus braços
Como naquela tardinha . . .
Não tardes, amor ausente;
Tem pena da minha mágoa,
Vida minha!

Wrap me lovingly
In the chain of your arms
As you did that evening . . .
Don't be long, my absent love,
Take pity on my pain
Life of mine!

"I went and had the dolphin tattoo done that same evening. The guy refused at first, he didn't do tattoos on women, I was too young, the skin on wrists is too thin, but I told him the whole story, in tears, and he eventually agreed. He didn't want me to pay."

I looked in silence at the dolphin as Manuela stroked it with her finger.

"I—I would never have known. You're so . . ."

"Don't, please. Without meaning to you're going to say something stupid and offensive."

I nodded. She was right. She smiled.

"You certainly don't have much luck with women. You're thinking: first a bitch, then a dike . . ."

"I—I never said that, Manuela."

"No, I'm saying it. Anyway, Delfina was the only girl I've ever loved, the only girl I've kissed and touched even. It was because it was her. Things aren't that straightforward, you see. I'll tell you an important truth which you might find useful: having luck with women doesn't exist. What does exist is knowing when a woman is giving you your chance, and seizing it. But you never see anything, Vincent. You should never have dared take my hand before I gave you a sign that meant yes, you can at least try."

I looked away.

"And there you go again, with your hangdog expression. You're—"

"Hopeless, is that what you were going to say?"

"I'm not that pessimistic anymore. But you're too on edge to spot the tiny signs. You project your longing for love onto some poor girl, and the effect this has is inevitably the exact opposite of what you're hoping. Because it's monstrous and clingy, that longing imposed on someone when they haven't done anything to provoke it. They want only one thing and that's to get away. And believe me, I know a lot about women."

She looked at her watch. "I have to go, I'm sorry. I'm already late."

"Can I call you? I'd like to."

"Sorry, Vincent, but I don't give out my number that easily. But we'll see each other again. Why don't you tell me how I can get hold of you. Do you have a business card?"

I started laughing and, slightly surprised by my reaction, Manuela laughed too.

The Ilbassan civilization on the high plateau of Holtepo has more gods than all other civilizations combined. Where some peoples might believe in a rain goddess and would dance to secure her favor, the Ilbassanians think there is a goddess for each raindrop. So they don't exhaust themselves jigging about over something so small.

I was translating this tale of Montestrela's when Irene called me. She was flying out in a few hours and just wanted to say goodbye. I initially thought of saying I was busy but didn't want to run away from the situation.

"I can come by your studio if you're working. I won't disturb you for long."

I hardly had time to tidy the place before Irene knocked on the door. She came in and with her came that heady, candy-smelling perfume. She was wearing her red dress and coral necklace.

"So this is where you live. It's not bad for someone who wants to write. It's light, not too out of the way. What a wonderful view . . ."

She walked over to the window and leaned on the top rail of the little balcony to look at the Tagus. I moved closer, slowly, until I was right behind her, I breathed in the smell of her, the sensual acidity of her sweat. Irene stood motionless, so did I.

I need only have taken one step and our bodies would have touched. Hers wouldn't have avoided mine, she would have leaned forward very slightly, and her buttocks would have moved back, pushing against my penis. I would have wanted her but wouldn't have done anything. Just pushed my body against hers until she felt me against her. She would have moved, gently, spread her legs, slowly. Her right hand would have touched my thigh, moved up toward my erection, she would have squeezed it through the fabric. She would have unbuttoned my jeans, they would have dropped to my ankles. I too would have slid my hand over her legs, touching her silky, milky skin, realizing with amazement she wasn't wearing anything under her dress. She would have bent over even further, offering herself, and, in that position, I would have taken her soft, moist cleft, my stomach smacking against her ass, my penis going back and forth inside her, harder and harder, without a single word spoken, looking at her buttocks but also, to avoid coming too quickly, the ferries on the Tagus. All at once she would have moved away, turned around, and knelt down. She would barely have licked the tip of my penis and cupped my balls before I ejaculated on her cheek and in her hair.

"You're right, it's a lovely view. If you lean out a bit, look, you can see the big statue of Christ the King. Can you see it?"

Irene left almost immediately. Her goodbye kiss landed on the corner of my mouth.

Her plane took off at eight o'clock and flew over Lisbon. I think I saw it.

DAY NINE

※

VINCENT

átia Moniz called me at about ten o'clock in the morning. The book was already done, the glue had dried, and even my cards were ready. Cátia Moniz. I really couldn't get used to it.

I stopped off at the hotel early. Antonio's bags were already in the lobby. He had found a seat on an afternoon flight to Mexico City. I had very little time left. I wanted him to come to the printers with me to pick up *Contos aquosos*. We agreed to meet for lunch near my studio and it was only as we were having coffee that I said: "By the way, I had Montestrela's book rebound at the printers on the rua da Barroca. It's weird: the girl who works there looks very much like Duck."

Antonio looked at me intently, took a deep breath.

"Okay, what are you playing at, Vincent? What have you been playing at this last week?"

"Nothing. It's the nearest place where you can have a book bound, I go there yesterday and I come across this woman—"

"Stop."

I thought he was going to punch me.

"Vincent . . . the day before yesterday, a picture. Today, book-binding. That's a lot of coincidences and a lot of chance occurrences."

"I promise you—"

"Why would you go stirring up shit like that? Isn't your own shit enough for you, that you have to go meddling in other people's? Do you really think that in the last ten years I haven't had time to track her and my son down? I'll tell you the whole story, because you're obviously dying to hear it, and then, then, listen to this, Vincent, you're going to pick up your fucking book from your fucking printers and you're going to leave her the hell in peace, and me too. Do you get it? Once and for all. Otherwise I'll break your legs, okay?"

"But—"

"Shut up."

WE'RE AT 42 rue Saint-Maur in Paris. It's the summer of 1974. A young woman has just come through the gate and under the porch. On her chest, in a baby carrier, she has a one-year-old boy, maybe a little older. When the concierge, who's cleaning the courtyard, asks who she wants to see, the woman says Flores, Antonio Flores, with a strong Portuguese accent. Second floor on the left.

Antonio knows nothing about what happened in Pragal, the birth, the hidden baby, the shame. In the chaos following Salazar's downfall, Duck must have run away to a distant relation in Paris. How she found his address, Antonio doesn't know either. It doesn't matter. She was never given the letters he'd written. He'd moved so many times that not all of those she'd written to him could have reached him. Duck climbs the stairs. She climbs quickly, she's in a hurry, she's carrying the child in her arms. There is no name on the left-hand door, just a Rolling Stones sticker shaped liked a mouth. The doormat is a hedgehog. She shows it to her baby, saying, "*Olha, Vitor, ouriço, ouriço.* Look, a hedgehog."

"*Riço,*" Vitor mimics.

Duck rings the bell but it's not working. She hesitates, then knocks on the door. It isn't Antonio who answers the door but a tall, flat-chested young woman with long blond hair, wearing a man's white shirt and jeans. She's pretty, she smiles kindly to the attractive girl on her doorstep and her tiny little boy. Duck starts to have her doubts. Was this really the second floor, do they count floors differently in France? She's not sure.

"Antonio Flores?" she asks.

Antonio? No, he's not here. This evening, yes. Come back. At about eight o'clock? Duck can't help seeing what the place looks like. It's a very small one-bedroom apartment, you can see the double bed from the door. She takes a step back. She feels cold. She shivers. Would she like to leave a message? No, she wouldn't. She doesn't want to write a single word that this girl could read. She goes back down the stairs, looks for the letterbox. Both names appear in the window: Antonio Flores—Agnès Mangin. *Idiota. Idiota.* She's put the baby back in his carrier, Vitor's so heavy already, she kisses his fine hair. Duck goes out onto the street, walks toward the blinding sun, almost running, still intoning *Idiota Idiota Idiota* in a hissing voice Vitor doesn't recognize.

When Antonio comes home and Agnès tells him that a pretty dark-haired girl came by with a baby, he gets it. Agnès gets it too. She leaves him. She doesn't leave him because he hid this woman and child from her, she leaves him because he abandoned them.

Antonio sets out to find Duck. Does he ever find her? Yes, but much later. Antonio is evasive about the dates, ambivalent. The truth would only prove his fickleness. In any event, Vitor is no longer a baby.

Duck says: If you're no longer you, I no longer want you. Those are the words. Antonio doesn't understand. How could he no longer be himself? She says exactly the same thing again. If you're no longer you, I no longer want you. He says: Don't say that, I love you. She replies that he has no concept about the words he's using. She also says that stains have permanently soiled the whiteness that they shared for many years apart, but that these years had added up because they'd been walking in opposite directions. She talks in metaphors, Antonio just tells her again that he loves her, he doesn't know what else to say. Oh, then he does: Vitor needs a father. You're wrong, she says, he has one now. He asks to see his son, their son. She corrects him: my son. Then, controlling herself, not softening but conciliatory: our son. She agrees, he can see him, because Vitor has a right to know, and she doesn't want any secrets. She also tells him she's pregnant, that she's happy to be having a child with the man she loves. Antonio cries, he cries over what could have been. She cries too, but in her case it's over what couldn't have been. They're not the same tears.

ANTONIO'S ANGER IS still there, very much alive, but the violence has dropped.

"So. There isn't a Duck anymore. There's Cátia Moniz, and she needs to be left alone."

"I didn't intend to—"

"I don't believe you. I don't know how you went about it, but you didn't go into that printers by chance. Who do you think you are to go inventing my destiny?"

I sighed. Of course. Antonio didn't want to go back to Duck any more than Ulysses did to Penelope. What is the *Odyssey* but the chronicle of an adventurer who loves Circe the magician and Calypso the nymph, who is promised the hand of Nausicaa, and who, despite appearances, constantly defers his homecoming? A man whom the gods forcibly deposit on the shores of Ithaca one night, and he's so angered by his fate that he engages in the most pointless and bloodthirsty of massacres, when merely uttering his name would have been enough to make all the suitors give way.

I didn't go to the airport with Antonio. We shook hands, coldly, and he climbed into a taxi. I bought *Le Monde* from the Santa Justa kiosk. It was two days old, dated September 20, and its leading article was about the *Rainbow Warrior*, the Greenpeace ship sunk by the French. At the bottom of the first page, an article by Umberto Eco reported Italo Calvino's death following a stroke on the night of September 18. Calvino was sixty-two years old. I had a naive but arresting thought: this man I had so often read would no longer write, his oeuvre was complete. There would never be another "latest book by Italo Calvino."

I went to pick up *Contos aquosos* from the printers. The book was waiting for me, it was beautifully done. I wanted to congratulate Cátia Moniz, but the tall guy at the till told me I should have been there in the morning, that she never worked Saturday afternoons.

"I'll let her know you're pleased with it, don't worry."

I didn't see her again.

$\mathcal{E}$ P I L O G U E

O ne of my tacit rules in a novel is that every door opened as the fiction unfolds should be closed at the very end. It is a sort of courtesy to the reader, for whom nothing should remain in the shade. Alas, this rule is very poorly matched with the realities of life, where nothing is so limpid, and nothing hermetically closed. But as I said this was a novel, I'll agree to comply with the rule, by rearranging the chapters which, until now, were in an arbitary order.

I've come across Antonio every now and then when I've gone to the newspaper. We have a relationship like co-workers, nothing more, but it has improved. He hasn't seen Irene again, she left the archive department for a job as an iconographer for a magazine, and the last time we talked about her he struggled to remember her name.

Vitor is growing up and looks like him. He still has a picture of him in his wallet. We never mention those nine days spent together, but, at his request, I gave him the charcoal portrait I did of Duck.

I've seen Irene three or four times on my annual trips to Paris. The last time we met, a sort of erotic game was instigated. I touched her breasts, they weren't as firm as they must have been a few years earlier. Two paltry victories.

Aurora left Lisbon for Berlin. I heard that she was awarded a European grant for the Arts and Culture, and she moved there. Antonio saw her face on a poster for a concert at the Salle Gaveau: the Wang-Oliveira duo. As for Karamazov, he fell under the spell of another young woman, a redhead who treated him badly.

Pinheiro died in prison in 1990 while serving a thirteen-year sentence for the murder of the grocer's wife. None of the other killings could be ascribed to him, and, as the saying goes, he took his secrets to the grave. Fate has not yet brought me in contact with Dr. Vieira, whose card I kept for a long time.

I ordered more furniture from Custódia as soon as I moved into a bigger apartment in the Castelo district. He never gave me a favorable price, quite the opposite. But he wasn't going to get rid of me that easily. I like to think that I'm the only person stopping him from closing his business. One time when he was telling me about his grandchildren, I asked whether he'd made them any wooden toys.

I've seen Manuela again, several times, always for lunch, never in the evening. The man she lives with, a very tall man with a beautiful, calm, regular-featured face, always says something to remind me how much he dislikes me.

My brother Paul got married. He has two boys I find unappealing and have no affection for, and he got divorced after five years. I didn't feel sorry for him, I thought his wife was a stupid, horse-faced woman. We don't see each other much.

Cátia Moniz—it doesn't make much sense to call her Duck now—has another daughter. I heard that from Custódia. But I lied earlier when I implied I hadn't seen her again. I didn't have new business cards made—I had more than one hundred and eighty left from my old address—but I saw her at the botanical gardens with her family. Vitor was pushing the baby's stroller and his little sister was pulling a toy behind her, a painted wooden duck with metal wheels. A duck. I smiled. I knew Custódia had made it, and I hoped he'd used off-cuts from my orders.

And then there's me: I translated the one thousand and seventy-three *Contos aquosos* but haven't found a publisher. The only one who showed any interest couldn't find anyone responsible for Jaime Montestrela's estate to sign the contract, and was worried there might be a court case after publication. Unless that was an excuse. As for the novel about Pescheux d'Herbinville, I never finished it, of course. I copied out my notes, but as the years went by, I lost interest in the project. I don't feel I need to apologize for that. I didn't make you any promises, as far as I know.

I haven't had any luck with women, or haven't known how to seize it if I did. Let's say the ones I liked didn't like me enough, and the ones I could have attracted were too ready to be attracted by pretty much anyone. Still, I'd have liked to have a child. Children. I'm sixty-five now and I'm not Picasso. The question stopped arising. There was never a Lena Balmer.

I may also know why Dad hanged himself. I'm growing steadily blind and, according to the doctor, it's a hereditary condition. This book is a result of that sense of urgency and terror, I've called it *Eléctrico W*—although the tramline no longer exists—and I don't know if it's good or bad. All bad novels are alike, but every good one is good in its own way.

And every day I look at the map of the Okavango Delta, that river that doesn't know how to find its way to the sea.

HERVÉ LE TELLIER is a writer, journalist, mathematician, food critic, and teacher. He has been a member of the Oulipo group since 1992 and one of the "papous" of the famous France Culture radio show. He has published fifteen books of stories, essays, and novels, including *Enough About Love* (Other Press, 2011), *The Sextine Chapel* (Dalkey Archive Press, 2011), and *A Thousand Pearls (for a Thousand Pennies)* (Dalkey Archive Press, 2011).

ADRIANA HUNTER studied French and Drama at the University of London. She has translated more than fifty books including *Enough About Love* by Hervé Le Tellier. She won the 2011 Scott Moncrieff Prize and has been short-listed twice for the French-American Foundation and Florence Gould Foundation Translation Prize. She lives in Norfolk, England.